Murder on Mt. Royal

Stephen E. Stanley

Murder on Mt. Royal

ISBN-10: 1466487194
ISBN-13: 978-1466487192

Printed in the United States of America.

Stonefield Publishing 2011

Also by Stephen E. Stanley

A MIDCOAST MURDER
A Jesse Ashworth Mystery

MURDER IN THE CHOIR ROOM
A Jesse Ashworth Mystery

THE BIG BOYS DETECTIVE AGENCY
A Jesse Ashworth Mystery

JIGSAW ISLAND
A novel of Maine

Author's Note:

This book is a work of fiction. All characters, names, institutions, and situations depicted in the book are the product of my imagination and not based on any persons living or dead. Anyone who thinks he or she is depicted in the book is most likely delusional and should be institutionalized.

Stonefield Publishing
Portland, Maine
StonefieldPublishing@gmail.com

Author's Web page: http://stephenestanley.com/

I'd like to thank my readers for their continued support and loyalty. I wrote my first book, *A Midcoast Murder,* as I was about to retire from thirty plus years of teaching and was looking for a creative outlet. It was a chance to start a new project and to actually finish one as well. It was also the chance to write the type of book I enjoy reading. When it was published I expected that maybe I'd sell forty copies or so to friends and relatives. To my surprise book sales took off and this book represents the forth in the Jesse Ashworth series.

I'd also like to thank Stonefield Publishing for taking a chance on an unknown writer. Small publishers such as Stonefield do not have the resources that big publishing companies have and do not have a full-time staff of copyreaders. Any typos or omissions are strictly my own. I'm a writer, not a typist. Anyone looking for editorial perfection should stick to the big publishers and pay accordingly.

I would also like to thank my partner Raymond Brooks for his continued support and dog sitting skills.

Stephen E. Stanley 2011

iv

Murder on Mt. Royal

Stephen E. Stanley

Cast of Characters

Jesse Ashworth—retired teacher and cookbook author with a newly minted detective license. After years working in New Hampshire, he has returned to his hometown of Bath, Maine and is now a private detective.

Argus—a five year old pug dog from Kentucky. He is Jesse's best friend and constant companion.

Tim Mallory—former police chief of Bath, Tim is co-owner with Jesse of the Bigg-Boyce Security Agency, nicknamed The Big Boys' Detective Agency by the locals.

Hugh Cartier—a Montreal police investigator. He asks for Jesse's help in investigating a murder. But is his interest in Jesse more than professional?

Chef David Boisvert—the head of the Culinary Institute of Montreal and a very unlikeable leader.

Candice Boisvert—the wife of the school's leader, she is in charge of the office.

Chef Robert Dube—the head of instruction at the cooking school.

Belinda Watkins—works in the culinary school office and has a plan that involves a hidden camera.

Armand LeBlanc—the head of security at the cooking school.

Maxwell Branch—a student at the Culinary Institute and Jesse's classmate. He and his wife run a bed and breakfast in Burlington, Vermont.

Jason Campbell—a late arrival on the scene.

Jenny Harris—a culinary student from New Hampshire where she and her husband plan to open a restaurant.

Rhonda Shepard—retired New Hampshire teacher, she taught with Jesse for over thirty years, then moved to Bath, and opened up a gift shop named Erebus. She loves vintage clothing and cake, not necessarily in that order.

Jackson Bennett—Jackson owns the largest insurance agency in Bath. He also is Rhonda Shepard's live-in boy friend.

Jason Goulet—Jesse's best friend. Jason, Tim, and Jesse went to high school together. Jason is married to Jesse's cousin Monica. Jason, at six foot seven, is a gentle giant.

Monica Ashworth-Twist Goulet—Monica married and went to Georgia to live until she divorced Jerry Twist. Like Jesse, she returned to Bath to begin a new life.

Billy Simpson—Billy and his ex-wife Becky were classmates of Jesse, Tim, and Jason. Billy finds mid-life to be challenging, but he is determined to find his place.

Jessica Mallory Cooper— Tim's daughter. She is a criminal justice graduate. She and her husband Derek work for the Bigg-Boyce Security Agency.

Derek Cooper— a Bath police officer and part-time agent in the Big Boy's Agency. He is Jessica's new groom.

Viola Vickner—a high priestess of the Wiccan faith, Viola works for Rhonda at Erebus.

Pastor Mary Bailey—the spiritual head of the liberal religious community, she is the pastor of All Souls' Unitarian Church in Bath.

Rabbi Beth White—Jesse's next door neighbor on Sagamore Street.

Beatrice Lafond—an English teacher at Morse High for many years, Old Lady Lafond still takes an interest in her former students even as she arrives at the century mark.

Parker Reed— the skipper of the windjammer *Doris Dean* out of Camden Harbor. Currently dating Billy Simpson, he and Jesse have a history which Parker makes known he wouldn't mind renewing.

*Montreal is a place not to be forgotten or mixed up in
the mind with other places, or altered for a moment in the
crowd of scenes a traveler can recall.*
- Charles Dickens

Chapter 1

The chef looked over my shoulder, "You are rolling that pastry too thin, Monsieur Ashworth," growled David Boisvert as he passed by my workstation. I took some shortening and spread in on the pastry, folded the dough in two and rolled it again. "And where did you learn that trick?" he asked.

"In culinary school in Paris," I shot back. "It makes the dough puff up more."

"Whatever!" replied the chef as he stomped off.

"Charming as always!" exclaimed Jenny Harris at the next workstation. "I'm just glad he's not our instructor, otherwise I don't think I'd bother to finish this cooking course."

"Chef Dube, on the other hand, is kind and supportive," joined in Maxwell Branch from another workstation.

"Which, I guess is why he is the instructor and not that Boisvert asshole," said Jenny.

"Do you have plans for lunch, Jesse?" Maxwell asked me.

"None. Why don't the three of us go to lunch in the Old City? I've had enough of cooking."

It was April in Montreal. Winter in Maine had seemed especially long, and I had a very bad bout of cabin fever. Don't get me wrong, I love my home, but I think I like going home better than staying home, if you know what I mean. It probably was my imagination, but all winter I had the feeling that I was being watched, and it felt good to have a change of scenery.

I rented a condominium in the Westmount section of Montreal from an elderly couple who decided to stay in Florida. They were neighbors of my parents in Fort Meyers, and they were quite happy to rent it to me for three or four months.

The condo was much larger than I needed, but it had a nice fenced in yard for my pug dog Argus, and several bedrooms for my Maine friends to come for a visit. I used the opportunity to take a cooking course with some other Americans at the Culinary Institute of Montreal. I was also taking a French language course at McGill University. Both courses were only a few hours a day, so I had plenty of free time as well.

"Lunch in the Old City sounds great!" said Jenny as she cut up some pastry dough. "I haven't had time to do much exploring."

"Me either," joined in Maxwell. "This is only the third day of class, and I've never been to Montreal before."

"But you're from Burlington," I said as I placed apple slices on the pastry. "The Vermont border is only about an hour away."

2

"I know. I'm just not a traveler." Maxwell was rolling out a square of chocolate piecrust. "How about you show us around and give us a tour?"

"That's a great idea," I answered.

"Can you take us up to the chalet on Mt. Royal?" asked Jenny. "I hear it's a great place for afternoon coffee. Maybe would could be there for four o'clock tea time."

"Sounds like fun." I said. Maxwell was nodding his head in agreement.

Chef Dube walked by as I was spreading an apricot glaze on my tart. He gave me an encouraging smile. "Very nice work, Jesse."

"Thank you chef!" I replied.

"Did you really go to culinary school in Paris?" asked Jenny.

"Sort of," I answered. "It was more of a culinary tour. But I did learn to make a decent beef burgundy."

We popped our creations in the ovens and then cleaned up our workstations while the pastries were baking. The institute donated the food we cooked to the local homeless shelter.

"Attention everybody!" announced Chef Dube. "When your pastries come out of the oven, put them on a rack to cool and meet me in the classroom, and we'll review today's lesson." We all filed out of the kitchen one by one.

The three of us hopped on the underground Metro and rode to the Old City section of

Montreal. I led the way, as I was most familiar with Montreal, having visited the city many times before. We found a small restaurant in an old stone building on a cobble stone street. It looked very European and exotic. We got a table by the window so we could watch all the comings and goings of the city.

Maxwell Branch was a short, wiry thirty-something who owned a bed and breakfast with his wife in Burlington, Vermont. Jenny Harris was in small woman in her forties who wanted to open a small restaurant in Concord, New Hampshire with her husband and grown son. I seemed to be the tallest and the oldest of the three.

"Are you guys going back home for the weekend?" I asked them both.

"Yes," answered Maxwell. "Weekends are the busiest for a B and B. I do the baking for the breakfasts."

"Me, too. Concord is only about four hours away," said Jenny. "And what about you? Bath, Maine is quite a drive isn't it?"

"Quite a drive is an understatement." I answered. "I have friends who will be coming for week-long visits while I'm here.

"When is Tim coming?" asked Jenny. Tim is the retired police Chief Timothy Mallory of the Bath, Maine Police Department. Tim and I share ownership of the Bigg-Boyce Security Agency, known locally as the Big Boys' Detective Agency. We share a personal relationship as well. We had gotten all our personal information shared and out of the way on our first day.

"Tim is coming up next week for a few days. He can only get away for a week at a time. My good friend Rhonda is coming for another week, and then my cousin Monica will be here as well. I have plenty of visitors lined up while I'm here."

The waitress came by and we ordered lunch. The menu had some great selections.

"Thank God the menus are in English," remarked Maxwell.

"Do you speak French at all?" Jenny asked me.

"No, I can catch a few words here and there, but that's it. My French course starts tomorrow, so hopefully I'll get better," I answered.

"I love Montreal!" said Maxwell. "It's so different."

"Me, too," I said. "I love the fact that the culture and language are so different, yet if I get overwhelmed I can speak English, look helpless, and I'll be understood."

"It is remarkable to hear everyone here switch from French to English so effortlessly," replied Jenny.

Our drinks arrived. "Have either of you talked much to our other class mates?" I asked. There were ten of us in the class. One of the students was from Nova Scotia. The other six members were from the mid-west. They were part of an elder hostel program on Quebec cooking. Maxwell,

Jenny, and I were the only New Englanders in the class, not to mention the only ones under sixty.

"Yes, they seem nice enough. Two of them are from somewhere in Ohio. One is from Chicago, and the rest are from Missouri." Jenny seemed well-informed.

"They're all staying in some dormitory situation, I think," added Maxwell.

"Is it the same dorm you two are in?" I asked. The culinary school had offered us several housing options. I had chosen my own.

"No," offered Jenny. "Our place is more like a rooming house. It's nice enough, but not too homey."

"You two will have to come over to my place some evening, just so you don't get cabin fever." I said. Just then our food arrived and it smelled heavenly.

"Has anybody figured out what the deal is with chef Boisvert?" Maxwell asked.

"He's the chief administrator of the school." I replied. I had read through the tedious information page on the school's web site. "Ms. Watkins in the office is the bookkeeper. Chef Dube is the head instructor and Chef Kelley and Chef Rondeau are assistant instructors."

"One would think," said Jenny between bites, "that the head administrator would have better things to do than run around the classrooms checking on everyone."

"He's a control freak!" hissed Maxwell.

"He is unpleasant." I agreed. "On the other hand, everything seems to be running well, and I'm learning a lot."

"I like the schedule," said Jenny. "We have afternoons off."

"Why don't we start the tour at my place later this afternoon? We can get in my car and I'll give you a tour. We can stop and have coffee somewhere along the way."

"I'm in! Maybe we could have coffee at the chalet on Mt. Royal? I've always wanted to see it up close," said Maxwell. He excused himself from the table to make a phone call.

"I'd love to see it, too! Let's plan to have coffee at the top around four this afternoon," suggested Jenny when Maxwell left the table. "How cool is it to have a mountain in the middle of the city?"

"How cool, indeed," I agreed.

****

Early April in Montreal gives little evidence of being spring. It was cold, the trees were bare, and there were patches of snow still on the ground. Maine wasn't much different, so I didn't feel like I was missing anything by being this far north.

I harnessed up Argus and we headed to the Atwater Metro station. The condo was several blocks away, but the streets could be confusing so I offered to meet Maxwell and Jenny at the subway stop.

Jenny waved to me as she and Maxwell emerged from the metro.

"You found your way on the metro okay?" I asked.

"Very easily," replied Maxwell. We turned and headed up the street.

"Did you notice the musical notes that the trains make when they take off?" I asked them.

"Yes, it sounded familiar, but I couldn't place it," said Jenny.

"*Fanfare for the Common Man*," I said.

"That's it!" replied Maxwell.

"It's really just the sound of the rubber wheels as the trains take off, but I love to hear it," I said. We turned up the next street and stopped at a red brick townhouse. "This is where I'm staying. Come on in and I'll show you around.

There were ten steps from the street level to the front door. I led them into a small hallway that opened into a large front parlor. "I thought it was a little over decorated when I moved in, so I packed up a lot of the old lady's bric-a-brac and put it in the basement," I explained as I showed them around.

"What a great kitchen!" exclaimed Jenny when I took them to the rear of the condo.

"The owners had it updated and remodeled just before they left for Florida. I think they may be planning to sell it sometime soon. There was a dining room here, but they tore out the wall to enlarge the kitchen."

"It's a great eat-in-kitchen," observed Maxwell.

"There are three bedrooms upstairs and that's about it. Check out the backyard." I said as I held the back door open. Argus crowded his way past us and rushed across the deck and down the steps to the grassy yard, where he lifted his leg against a tree.

"Wow!" exclaimed Maxwell. "Brick walls and even a fountain. You'd never know you were in the city

"Anyone for a glass of wine?" I asked.

"I'm in!" answered Maxwell.

"Me, too," replied Jenny looking at her watch, "Just so we have coffee at the top of the mountain at four."

"Why four?' I asked.

"I want to hear the church bells of the city from up there when they ring the hour."

"That would be fun," I agreed.

After drinks we got into my car and I drove them around the city. I started down Rue Ste Catherine and then looped back through some of the more interesting neighborhoods. I gave a good tour if I do say so myself. I made sure to mention the metro stops as we went along so that they could explore on their own later. I saved Mt. Royal for last since it was closest to Westmount.

"It seems strange to have a place like this in the middle of the city," observed Maxwell as we drove past St Joseph's Oratory, past the Catholic and Protestant cemeteries and on to Mt Royal Park.

"It does make Montreal unique in that way for sure," I said. "I tried walking up the trail from McGill University once, but it was far too steep. It's much easier in a car.

I brought Argus up here yesterday for a walk and he loved it."

"I can see why," said Jenny from the back seat. "I hate to mention it, but I really need to go to the bathroom"

"Me too," agreed Maxwell as he checked his watch. We approached a small building along the road. I pulled the car into the small parking lot and Jenny and Maxwell jumped out.

"Are you coming?" asked Maxwell.

"I'm good," I replied and used the time to tune around the radio dial.

We drove along the winding road up the mountain and passed many people going on late afternoon walks.

We were rounding a corner near the top when a runner dressed in running gear jumped out in front of us from the bushes and took off at top speed. I slammed on the brakes to avoid hitting him. He kept on running and disappeared down the road.

"Wasn't that..." I began.

"Chef Dube, I'm sure," finished Jenny from the back seat.

"It sure looked like him," said Maxwell.

"What was he doing out here, I wonder," I said to my car mates.

Chapter 2

In a few weeks Montreal's spring would be breaking out in colorful tribute to the season, but for now the landscape was bleak with only a few hints of the season to come. My two companions and I continued on our drive up the mountain.

Mount Royal is the most recognizable landmark in the city. Atop the mountain is a lighted cross that is 103 feet high, placed there in 1924. The first cross on the mountain was erected in 1643 by Paul Chomedey de Maisonneuve, the founder of the city. I guess in other words you could say that Montreal was very, very old.

We reached the chalet exactly at four o'clock and bought coffee and pastries and sat at a table with a view out over the city of Montreal. We really could hear the church bells from where we sat.

"You really get a sense of the size of the city from up here," remarked Jenny sipping her coffee.

"I'll bet it's really beautiful in the summer," added Maxwell.

"I'd love to see this view after a snow storm," I said. We finished our tea and it was time to go.

As we headed up back down the mountain we ran into a road block. There were police cars with lights flashing. Several of the cars were Montreal police and some were RCMP. I was disappointed to note that the Mounties were wearing ordinary uniforms, not the tight red uniforms from old movies.

One especially good looking police officer was waving us to stop with his flashlight.

"Someone should tell him that it's still daylight," I muttered. I rolled down my window.

"I'm sorry, but I need to ask you to turn around and exit the park in the other direction. There's been an incident." He spoke English without an accent.

"An incident?" I asked.

"Yes, I'm afraid so."

"How did you know to speak to me in English and not French?" I asked the good-looking cop.

"The Maine license plate was a clue. Did you see anything unusual on your drive up here?"

"Not really. It's all very unusual for a visitor."

"I suppose it is. Here's my card if you think of anything."

"Thanks," I said. I rolled up the window and turned the car around.

"I wonder what that was all about?" asked Maxwell Branch from the back seat.

"Very curious," agreed Jenny Harris, who was riding shotgun.

Having nothing else to show them in this part of town, I drove them back toward St. Joseph's Oratory, which claims to be the largest church in Canada. Since none of us happened to be catholic, it seemed strange and imposing and just a bit alien.

13

The church started as a small chapel in 1904 when Brother Andre dedicated it to St. Joseph. Over the years it has grown and was finally completed in 1967. The oratory is purported to be a place of healing and there are thousands of crutches on display from those who were allegedly healed. Brother Andre had recently become a saint and there were photographs of the oratory's celebration on display.

"What's that?" asked Jenny pointing to a red panel of glass in one of the smaller chapels of the basilica.

"That's Brother Andre's heart," I replied.

"Okay then," said Maxwell as he started looking for the nearest exit.

After drinks at a Westmount bar, I dropped Maxwell and Jenny off at their lodging and headed back to Westmount. Argus was glad to see me, and I decided to call the office before I settled down.

"Bigg-Boyce Security," said the voice on the other end of the phone.

"Some security business," I answered. "You didn't check caller ID."

"Hi step-dad," answered Jessica Cooper. Jessica is Tim's daughter who is now married to police officer Derek Cooper of the Bath police department. Jessica runs the office and Derek works for us part time.

"Men of a certain age…" I began to say.

14

"...are too old to be called step-dad. I've heard it all before," said Jessica. This was a game we played every few weeks. I adore Jessica. She's the most together young woman I know.

"Is the old man around?" I asked.

"Oh yes. He's been driving me crazy since you left. You need to take him with you next time."

"Suck it up kid. He's your dad."

Jessica put my call through.

"How's it going?" asked Tim.

"And I miss you, too," I replied, a bit annoyed that he sounded like he was talking to one of our agents.

"Oh, Jesse," said Tim. "I didn't realize it was you."

"Fire the receptionist."

"I can't. She works for peanuts. How are you?"

"Cooking class is fun, though one of the chefs is a pain in the ass. I start French class tomorrow."

"Have fun. I'll be up next week. Business is slow here. How's Argus?"

"Argus is sitting in my lap as we speak." We talked for a few more minutes and then I hung up. It was good to hear his voice.

****

The next morning I put the coffee on to brew and walked to the corner and bought a copy of *The Gazette*, Montreal's English newspaper. I wasn't ready yet to tackle written French. One article caught my eye, and I was halfway through the

15

news story when my cell phone rang. It was Maxwell Branch.

"Jesse, did you see the TV news this morning?"

"No, but I've just read about it in the paper."

"Chef Boisvert was found murdered on Mt. Royal!"

"I'm guessing that was the 'incident' that closed the road yesterday."

"Do you think Chef Dube was involved?"

"Why would he be involved?" I asked and then remembered that we had seen him running from the area on Mt. Royal. "Oh, yes. I'm sure it was just a coincidence."

"Should we tell the police?"

"Probably," I answered. "That cop gave me his card yesterday. I'll give him a call."

"And I'm supposed to tell you that classes for the rest of the week have been canceled. In the mean time we are suppose to read ahead in the textbook."

****

Lieutenant Hugh Cartier showed up on my doorstep shortly after I placed the call. Today he wasn't wearing a uniform, but was dressed in a fairly flattering suite and I couldn't decide if I liked this look or the uniform look better. I showed him my investigator license, and unlike the Maine police, he seemed somewhat impressed.

"What can you tell me about yesterday, Dr. Ashworth?"

"Please call me Jesse, lieutenant."

"If you call me Hugh."

I gave him a brief account of attending the cooking school and how we knew the victim. Then I told him how we had seen Chef Dube jogging on Mt. Royal.

"I'm sure it was just a coincidence," I added.

"Do you believe in coincidences, Jesse?"

"No, I don't actually."

"Neither do I. The question is what was Dube doing there? So tell me what you've observed."

"Chef Boisvert seemed to be the one in charge of the business end of the school. I got the distinct impression that he was hard to work with. Or to be blunt, we all thought he was an asshole. Chef Dube appears to be in charge of instruction and oversees the other instructors. There are four other instructors as well. Chef Boisvert's wife Candice runs the office with office manager Belinda Watkins, and there is Armand LeBlanc who is the security officer."

"Is that the entire staff?"

"I think there is a cleaning crew that comes in at night, though I've never seen them."

"Well, I'm going to have to have a word with Dube. It would be helpful if you keep your eyes and ears open and let me know what you observe."

"Sure thing," I replied. All the time we were talking Argus was sitting in my lap looking at

Hugh and wagging his tail. I had to hold him back as I didn't think Lieutenant Cartier would appreciate dog hair on his navy blue suite.

"So you're new in town?"

"Yes, though I've been visiting here over the years. I love Montreal."

"I know this great little restaurant in the Latin Quarter. I'll give you a call and maybe we can have dinner while you tell me what you've observed at the school. Thanks for your help." And he got up and left.

"What just happened here?" I asked Argus, but he just wagged his tail.

****

With the rest of the morning free, I harnessed up Argus and we took a walk in the neighborhood. I was feeling a little lost and missed my usual home routine. Argus seemed to have adapted well to the move and was enjoying the walk. Lots of new smells for him, I guess. Spring was still rather bleak here and it was chilly, but here and there were daffodils that added a bit of color to the landscape, and I noticed that the grass was beginning to green up.

We returned back to the house where I made a sandwich and got ready for my French class at McGill.

Chapter 3

C lasses resumed two days later, but the school was hardly back to normal. Candace Boisvert was absent, which was understandable under the circumstances. Ms. Watkins had arrived at work, but left early. Chef Dube had given the class over to the assistant instructors and we were presently in the classroom reviewing the finer points of marinating meat.

Chef Rondeau was treating the subject as if it was the most important thing in the world. His heavy French accent was tiring on the ears after a few minutes. Maxwell Branch looked at me and made a rude gesture with his hand, and Jenny Harris rolled her eyes. Some of the other students had a glazed look on their faces. Clearly Chef Rondeau was in his own little world.

Finally we were let loose in the kitchen for some hands-on experience. Today we were given different assignments to create a lunch for the class. My assignment was to make rice pilaf. Not a very challenging task to my way of thinking.

We were all working diligently at our workstations when we heard a commotion and a band of police officers swarmed the school. The raid was led by Lieutenant Hugh Cartier, this time in uniform. We were herded back into the classroom to be questioned later. From the classroom we heard a commotion and I got up and watched from the door.

One officer walked past the door carrying what looked like a bloody knife inside a plastic bag. In a minute or two I saw Lieutenant Hugh Cartier lead Chef Dube away in handcuffs. It didn't take a genius to figure out what happened.

Armand LeBlanc, the school's security guard, was following behind another officer. He wasn't in handcuffs, but I wasn't sure what his role in all this was.

Lieutenant Cartier returned and questioned us as a group. He informed us that indeed the newspaper reports were true and that Chef Boisvert had been stabbed to death and had we noticed anything unusual on the day of the murder?

Everyone agreed that there had been some type of tension in the air, but I have a hard time keeping my mouth shut and pointed out that was hardly any type of evidence. Of course suddenly all eyes were on me.

"Well," began Cartier, "you are lucky to have a private detective in your class." The whole class looked at me. Only Jenny and Maxwell knew that I worked for the Bigg-Boyce Agency.

"Do I detect a note of verbal irony in your voice, lieutenant?" Bring it on Cartier! To my surprise Cartier smiled.

"Not at all, Dr. Ashworth. I'm hoping you might remember some details."

"Well," I answered, somewhat mollified, "feelings aside, I saw what I'd describe as an animated conversation between Chef Dube and

Chef Boisvert. I couldn't hear what was being said, but the tone was confrontational."

"Well if any of you think of anything, anything at all, give us a call." We were dismissed. The police investigators were going over the school looking for clues. As I was leaving Hugh Cartier stopped me.

"Are you free for dinner later?" he asked. I hesitated briefly. "I'd just like to pick your brains about this case."

"I have nothing planned."

"I'll pick you up at six then."

****

Argus seemed to know that I was planning to go out. He followed me around the house and wouldn't let me out of his sight. I was dressed and had just finished talking with Tim on the phone. I had told him about the murder and the arrest of Chef Dube.

"Why are there always dead bodies whenever you get involved in something?"

"Bad timing, I guess. What's happening at the agency?"

"We installed two new burglar alarms this week. Other than that nothing new here."

"When are you coming up?"

"Early next week, Jessica and Derek can look after the business for a few days."

"Can't wait," I said. "I miss you."

21

"I miss you, too. But you're having a good time?"

"Except for the murder. I'm not sure what's going to happen to cooking school. But I'm enjoying my French class."

I didn't bother to tell him about my impending dinner with Hugh Cartier. I'd save that for later.

Exactly at six o'clock the door bell rang, and Argus went tearing off to greet the visitor. Hugh Cartier was standing on my doorstep, and I must add that he cleans up real good. Hugh is my height, about six feet tall, has broad shoulders and a great jaw line. I couldn't tell his age other than to say that middle age had arrived only to add character to his face.

"Come in. You remember Argus?"

"Hi little guy." Argus was beside himself with excitement. Argus is my barometer for visitors. The dog can sense if someone is genuine or not. I never trust anyone who doesn't like dogs, and if Argus is anything less than excited by a visitor, well, it's a warning.

"Would you like a drink? I've got wine and beer."

"A beer would be great."

"Let's go sit in the living room."

"You look different when you're not on duty."

"Thanks, I think. You look good dressed up, too."

"So where are you taking me?" I asked to change the subject.

"I thought you might like to try some authentic French Canadian cuisine."

"Sounds good to me.

"This is a nice house," remarked Hugh, looking around the room. Argus was sitting in his lap and being petted.

"It belongs to friends of my parents. They decided to stay in Florida"

"Lots of winters I'd like to be in Florida."

"Yes, I understand Canada can be quite cold in winter."

"That's an understatement if I ever heard one." Hugh looked at his watch. "We really should get moving. The restaurant is very popular."

Hugh led me out to his parked BMW, which made me think that policemen in Montreal must be paid better than those back home. We drove through the various neighborhoods of Montreal to the Latin Quarter located near the University of Quebec. The streets were teaming with pedestrians, many of whom appeared to be students. Hugh found a parking spot and eased his car in.

"Montreal has some great restaurants," said Hugh as he led me to a nearby eatery.

"I've already tried *poutine,*" I replied, referring to their fries topped with gravy and cheese curds.

"We have much more than *poutine.*"

We entered a small restaurant with lots of candles and ferns placed along the dark paneled walls. The head waiter apparently knew Hugh and rushed over to give him a hug. They spoke briefly in French, and I was only able to catch a word here and there. The waiter, whose name I learned was Maurice, seated us in a quiet corner near a window. We had a good view of the street. Even at this early hour the restaurant was nearly full.

Maurice brought us menus that were in French with English translations in very small print underneath. Because of the small print and the dark room, I had to pull out my reading glasses to see.

"This place specializes in both British and French Canadian cuisine," offered Hugh. I noticed that he, too, had pulled out a pair of reading glasses. I ordered Jiggs dinner, which was the special of the day, and a glass of Molson. Hugh ordered the same.

"Across the border," I remarked, "we call it New England boiled dinner." Basically it was corned beef, cabbage, potato, carrots, and turnip. The Canadian version differed only in the addition of turnip greens or yellow peas.

"So I imagine," he replied. "Let's talk about the cooking school."

"Sure thing. What can I tell you?"

"Don't you find it just a little too convenient that the murder weapon was found in Robert Dube's locker?"

"Actually that was my first thought. He would have to be stupid to hang on to a murder weapon, let alone keep it in his work locker."

"Also, there was no attempt to wipe off the blood." Hugh added.

"Which means that whoever planted the weapon is the killer, and that the killer is someone who is familiar with the school."

"And I think that Chef Dube might be innocent."

"Then why did you arrest him?"

"On the surface the evidence points to him. And arresting him may put the real killer at ease and make him or her become careless."

"Also," I added, "Robert Dube could be guilty and just not too bright."

"There is that to consider, too."

Our meals arrived and I have to say that it was one of the best boiled dinners I had ever had. I suspected that beer may have been substituted for water in the boil at some point. I'd have to try it out at home sometime.

"What I'd like you to do," said Hugh between bites, "is to do a little bit of snooping around when you're at the school. I suspect that there is more going on than just cooking classes. We can offer you a small stipend."

"Ah," I said. "I was wondering why you were taking me to dinner just to interview me."

"You think I invited you to dinner just for business?" He was staring at me now.

"Well…" I stammered.

"Anything wrong with making new friends? Being a policeman is a lonely job."

"Yes, I know. My partner Tim is a former police chief."

"But he's not here with you now is he?"

"No, he's back home running the business. He'll be here for the weekend, though."

"I'd like to meet him," said Hugh in a tone that made me doubt his sincerity.

"So what is it exactly you want me to do?" I asked to change the subject.

"I'd like you to just nose around and see how people at the school get along. Try to pry some gossip from some of the workers. And use your own judgment for the rest."

"That sounds reasonable," I agreed.

The rest of the dinner we talked about our backgrounds. I learned that Hugh Cartier had been married and divorced and had two grown sons, now in college. He had worked for the Montreal Police for over twenty years and was looking forward to retirement. I told him about teaching high school for thirty years and then taking over the Bigg-Boyce security Agency with Tim.

After a dessert of *crème Brule* Hugh drove me home. As I was about to get out of the car Hugh reached over and ran his hands through my hair.

"I'd like to see you again," he said.

Now let's be honest. I'm well into middle age with plenty of gray at the temples. I'm six feet tall, which is about an inch shorter that most men I know. And I really don't consider myself a model, and though people tell me I'm very good looking, I think they're just being kind. Tim Mallory, on the other hand, is a ten plus. So, I thought it unlikely that a good looking Canadian of a certain age was going to be interested in me that way. And what is it with guys running their fingers through my hair?

"Sure," I said. "I'll let you know what I find out at the school."

Argus was waiting for me when I got back inside the house. He was wagging his curled up tail.

"Well, Argus, that was an interesting evening." His answer was to lick my face.

Chapter 4

Yet again cooking class was delayed for a day and then we were back at our workstations. I was in the middle of cutting up a chicken when Chef Kelley walked by and gave me an encouraging word. We were making the Canadian version of chicken pie. I had already chopped of the vegetables and was about ready to tackle the pie crust. Making pie crust is not one of my culinary gifts.

We were encouraged to rotate workstations since they were all configured differently. I was told it was so the students would have practice in different setting. I suspected it was more about money. Today I was next to Jeff Taylor, the only Canadian in the class. He came from New Brunswick where he taught school. He and I were sharing war stories from the classrooms. Of course my stories were more interesting if I do say so myself.

"I was teaching a journalism class with a lesson unit on libel and slander. One of my students used the term 'defecation of character' instead of 'defamation of character' in her essay. I rather liked it," I said.

"If only we had all started to write them down, we'd have a book," he replied.

"People would think we were making up the stories."

"That's true."

"So," I said as I lowered my voice, "what do you think is going on here?"

"I'm not sure, but there is something fishy here, I can tell you that. I went to high school with Robert Dube and he's no killer."

"You went to high school with Chef Dube?" I asked. This was news to me. I wondered if Hugh Cartier knew this.

"Yes, though it was a long time ago, and we really weren't close. But when I learned he was part owner of a cooking school, I decided to contact him and come here for classes."

"Isn't your school still in session?" I asked as I realized that it was only April.

"I took this semester off because I'll be teaching summer school."

It was time to tackle the pastry, so Chef Kelley gathered us around his work station, which was fitted out with overhead mirrors so we could see him work from several angles. He made it look easy, but I dreaded having to go back and try it on my own.

As we started back to our stations Chef Rondeau came into the classroom to make an announcement.

"The medical examiner has released Chef Boisvert's remains. His funeral will be tomorrow afternoon. We are not cancelling classes because we know you have lost several days of class already. You are all welcome to attend the funeral in the afternoon after class."

It became quiet as we all remembered that there had been a tragedy and that we had all met the victim.

My pie crust turned out okay, and I assembled the chicken pie and put in the oven. I must say that it looked yummy. I took the opportunity to take a trip to the men's room which took me past the offices. Candace Boisvert was not at her desk, which was understandable under the circumstances, but Belinda Watkins was in Candace's office going through her file cabinets. She saw me and immediately closed the drawer and left with a folder.

"Just needed to get some records," she said to me with a slight French accent as she passed by. I thought that was odd as it was really none of my business. On my way back to the classroom I saw that the door to the security office was closed and I could hear voices. I looked around making sure no one was watching and stepped closer to the door. I recognized the voice of Candace Boisvert arguing with Armand LeBlanc, the security guy. They were speaking in French, so I gave up any hope of understanding what they were saying, but it was clear by the tone and volume that all was not well.

When I got back to class everyone was milling around, waiting for their pies to be done. I checked in with Maxwell and Jenny. We made plans to go to the botanical gardens later in the week. Chef Kelley suggested that we all taste one of the pies and then send the rest to the local soup kitchen. We all agreed, and I have to say that the pie recipe was delicious. I couldn't wait to make it when I got home.

Home! I'd been so busy that I hadn't given much thought to home. Home was a 1920's yellow bungalow named Eagle's Nest that I restored several years ago. The garden would be just showing some green about now. Tim would be at the office all day and then go home to an empty house. For a moment I felt guilty about being away, but when I thought about how exciting Montreal was, I got over it.

Everyone had left the cooking school as it was approaching noontime. I lingered behind, pretending to do some research in the small library. It was nothing more than a large closet with bookshelves stuffed with cookbooks. When I noticed that Candice Boisvert and Armand LeBlanc had left for lunch, I stepped outside and looked into the office area. Belinda Watkins, the office manager was nowhere in sight. I casually walked up to her desk and touched the mouse on the computer. The screen saver gave way to a view of the computer desktop, and I saw several file folders that were labeled school files. I reached in my pocket and took out my thumb drive and stuck it into one of the USB sockets and began to copy the file folders.

It takes a while to copy files and I was getting nervous about being in the office should someone return. As soon as the file downloads were completed, I pulled the thumb drive out and went back to the library just as the door flung open and Armand Leblanc returned. I took out my notebook and started copying a recipe. Armand saw me and stopped by the library.

"Are you finding everything you need?" he asked.

"Yes, I think I've got what I need."

I got off at the Atwater Metro station and stopped at a sandwich shop and picked up a ham and cheese sub to take home for lunch. Ironically taking cooking classes all morning made me not want to cook when I got home.

Argus was glad to see me, and I harnessed him up for a walk and took my sandwich along. We walked up to a nearby park. It was one of the first really warm days and the weather had brought people to the park. I found a bench to sit on and pulled Argus up to sit beside me while I ate my sandwich. Argus sat quietly watching me eat and hoping I'd drop something, but he knew that if he waited patiently for me to finish, he'd be rewarded with a doggie treat.

People walked by giving us admiring glances, but I knew it was Argus they were looking at and not me. I sighed. Thirty years ago it would have been me they looked at, but now I was just another invisible middle aged man sitting on a park bench. Two more days and Tim would be up to spend the week. In fact everyone I know back in Bath had promised to come up for a visit. I certainly wouldn't be lonely this spring. I'd be back home for the summer before I know it.

I gazed around at all the brick buildings around me and at Mt. Royal, which seemed to dominate the city. I remembered our trip up Mt. Royal the other day and that it might be a good idea to go up and check out the area just to see where Chef Boisvert was killed. I looked at my watch and I still had two hours before my French class. I always felt drained after class. It seems to take a lot of energy to study a language. I gave Argus his treat and we continued on our walk. Suddenly, I had the feeling that I was being watched, though it must have been my imagination.

****

The church was full for the funeral. I expected we'd be attending a catholic service in French and was surprised that the service was in an English-speaking Anglican church. That just proved to me that you can't make assumptions about people based on their names. Our class all sat together at the back of the church. It was finally dawning on us that this was a case of murder and that somehow we were all affected just by our participation in the culinary school.

I was finding it hard to focus on the funeral. Not that that was surprising since I'm convinced that I suffer from adult attention deficit disorder. I was beginning to feel claustrophobic and decided to go to my happy place. I closed my eyes and was on a Hawaiian beach with an umbrella drink in my hand and lots of pretty surfer boys riding the waves. I must have dozed off because the next thing I knew Maxwell Branch poked me with his elbow and we were standing up to leave the service.

"Have a nice nap?" asked Maxwell.

"Lovely, thank you."

"You were snoring," accused Jenny as she pulled up on the other side of me.

"Did I miss anything?"

"God, no," answered Maxwell.

"Let's grab some lunch," suggested Jenny.

"I'm starved," agreed Maxwell.

"I know just the place," I said.

Chapter 5

Montreal's China town is small by big city standards, but there was no mistaking the area. The large Asian gate gave way to a small section of the city heavy with Chinese decorations. I took them to a small Chinese restaurant that I had discovered on one of my previous trips. Maxwell and Jenny had never been here before so we did some sightseeing before heading down to the restaurant that was situated below street level. The restaurant had low ceilings and was made up of several small rooms. We were seated near a window, which meant that we could look up and see people's feet as they passed by.

We were given menus written in both French and English, and we each ordered a combination plates. I poured tea for everyone from the steaming tea pot, and we sat back and relaxed.

"Did anyone notice anything strange about the funeral?" I asked.

"Now that you say it, yes," Jenny seemed to be warming her hands with the tea cup.

I turned to Maxwell, who just shrugged his shoulders. "It didn't seem to me," he slowly said, "that any one was too upset. I didn't see any tears."

"That's exactly what I was thinking," I replied and Jenny nodded her head in agreement. "And the wife kept checking her watch as if she were late for an appointment."

"That's cold," agreed Jenny. "I don't recall seeing the office person either. You know, Belinda whats-her-name."

Our food arrived and we ate in silence for a few minutes as we dug into our meal.

"I just realized what's been bothering me." They both stopped eating and looked at me. "No one seemed surprised by the murder. It's almost like everyone expected it." As I said it I knew it was true. I could tell from Maxwell and Jenny's face that they knew it too.

After lunch we walked over to the gothic revival edifice of Notre Dame. The stone church looked like it had been dragged out of Europe stone by stone and reassembled here near *Place d'Armes*. We paid our admission and entered the church.

"What type of church charges admission?" complained Maxwell as we stepped into the huge edifice. "I'd like to…" and the words died on his lips as he looked up toward the sanctuary.

"Oh my," gasped Jenny was we looked around at one of the most striking churches in North America

****

"I didn't see it at first," I said. Hugh Cartier had booth hands on my shoulders and was leaning over me to get a better look at the screen.

"You stole the files off the computers?"

"Of course not," I answered. "The files are still there. I merely copied a few items and put them on my thumb drive. Nothing is missing, and stealing is such an ugly term." I didn't know anything about Canadian law, but I was guessing that even in the best scenario this would be in a gray area.

"We won't be able to use this in court," he said. I was very aware that his fingers were stroking the back of my neck. I considered telling him to stop, but the urge passed as his fingers massaged my stiff neck. I clicked on the file icon. It was a video file and then the screen was full of action. What Hugh saw on the screen made him take his hands off me and stand bolt upright.

There on the screen was Candice Boisvert with her tongue halfway down Armand LeBlanc's throat. They were in her office next to Belinda Watkins's desk. After a few seconds the scenario switched to a much more adult activity.

"That must be tough on the knees," I remarked.

"And this was on Belinda's computer?"

"Yes, though I've no idea why she would want to watch this. It isn't exactly tasteful," I added.

"Something is really wrong at that school."

"No shit! And I've only scratched the surface."

"I owe you dinner for this," he said. I looked at Hugh to see if I saw any hint of anything, but he just gave me a blank look. "There's a great beer and burger place around the corner."

"Okay, sounds good. In fact I was hungry and I hadn't thought to buy anything for dinner.

"So Tim's coming to visit you tomorrow," said Hugh between beer sips. The Irish pub was near the house, and it was a pretty good facsimile of an actual Irish watering hole. Hugh had a good Irish stout, and I settled for pale ale.

"Yes, he'll be here for a week or so."

"I can't wait to meet him." I wasn't sure that was such a good idea. Tim was so good looking he could get a straight guy to switch teams after a couple of drinks, and if my suspicions were correct Hugh Cartier wouldn't need the drinks at all.

"He was a cop for twenty-five years; you'll have a lot in common."

"We already do," he said mysteriously and lifted his glass to me.

"Why do you think Belinda had that video?" I asked to change the subject.

"What three reasons are there for most crimes?" he shot back at me.

I thought about it for a moment. "Money, revenge, and love."

"You're right. Or any combination of those three."

"How did she get the video?" I asked. "I'm sure they didn't let her stand there with a video camera."

"If you noticed the quality of the video, you saw that it was low resolution. It was probably one of those small computer cams. No one would notice it on a crowded desk."

Just then our burgers arrived. Hugh was already putting vinegar on his fries while I reached for the catsup bottle.

****

It was Saturday and with no classes to attend I did some basic housework and went shopping for groceries. Tim would most likely arrive in the late afternoon. The drive was over six hours from Bath to Montreal, and though Tim never drove over the speed limit on back roads, he would drive at a steady pace and make good time.

I swear Argus knew something was up because at first he followed me around the house, and then he kept staring at the door, as if he expected someone to show up. I sometimes think dogs are more psychic then humans.

Speaking of psychic, there was something nagging at me about the Boisvert case. I hadn't heard any more about Chef Dube since his arrest. Cartier hadn't said anything about him and as far as I knew he didn't have a motive for murder. Something didn't fit.

I was busy in the kitchen making the chicken pie we studied at school. Tim would want to know how classes were going so I decided I show him. The only thing I changed was the pie crust. I used a biscuit mix to make the top crust and didn't feel the least bit guilty about it either.

Argus began to pace and whine, so I looked out the window and saw Tim unloading his car in front of the house. I opened the door and Argus went flying past me. Tim dropped his suitcase and caught Argus who was yelping in delight.

"I think he's saying that he missed you." I grabbed the suitcase while Tim carried Argus into the house. I sat the suitcase down and gave Tim a big hug. "And I missed you as well."

"At least here you're surrounded by new things to see and do. Back home everything is empty without you."

"Well, brace yourself, because you are going to have one busy week."

I went into the kitchen and poured out two glasses of wine. Tim followed me around.

"This is a nice place," he observed. "Not really your style, but nice in its own way."

"I have a style?"

"Yes, you certainly do."

"Come on up and I'll show you the upstairs."

"I thought you'd never ask," said Tim unbuttoning his shirt as he followed me to the bedroom.

I was peacefully lying back on the pillows when I heard the kitchen buzzer go off. "Shit!" I said as I jumped up, grabbed my underwear, and ran for the kitchen. I was sure that the pie would be burnt, but when I pulled it out of the oven the crust was golden and the pie was bubbling. I picked up two pot holders and moved the pie to a cooling rack and went back to the bedroom to finish dressing. Tim was already dressed and unpacking his things.

"You didn't bring a lot of clothes," I observed as he unpacked.

"I'm planning to shop for clothes while I'm here."

"That's an excellent idea. Your wardrobe could use a little zing. Dinner will be ready when you come down."

"Thanks."

I spooned out the chicken pie and we ate in the kitchen with Argus at our feet. I had kept Tim up to date on the Boisvert case during our nightly phone calls, but I filled him in on yesterday's events.

"Just so you know," said Tim with a gleam in his eye. "Buying you dinner is not standard police procedure."

"Maybe it's a Canadian thing," I shot back.

"I can't wait to meet this Cartier person. He better be old and ugly."

"He's neither, but I'm sure you'll like him."

"We'll have to see about that."

"So what do you think about the video?"

"I think that it's blackmail. Did Cartier say what he was going to do with the information you gave him?"

"I got the impression he was hanging tight to see what other things would turn up."

"That's what I would do. This is very good by the way. You pick this up in school?"

"Yes I did."

"And how is your French coming along?"

"Well, that seems to be coming along slower than my cooking, but I'm getting better at reading signs. What's the news from home?"

"Parker Reed has moved in with Billy Simpson."

"I'm glad, Billy needs some stability in his life" Parker Reed was an old flame of mine. He's recently been promoted to captain of the *Doris Dean*, a Maine Windjammer out of Camden. I worked as the ship's cook one summer when the real cook took a powder in the middle of the voyage. Billy Simpson was one of my classmates back at Morse High. He's had a rough time since his wife's breakdown and the subsequent divorce.

"You think this will be good for Billy?" Tim asked.

"Parker Reed has a roving eye and busy hands, and will probably try to hit on every guy in sight, but as long as he's nice to Billy, I think it will be okay."

I looked carefully at Tim. Back in high school he was handsome, but as he aged he got better looking. The lines on his face only enhanced his laughing eyes and strong jaw. He was one of those lucky guys who never has to work out, yet has muscles and abs to die for. I, on the other hand, have to walk every day just to stay under two hundred pounds.

"You look good," I observed.

"Lack of stress. It helps to be retired. And you're looking pretty healthy yourself."

"How's business?"

"No cases to investigate, so it's just security work. We've added two new alarm accounts, and I've have an idea I want to pass by you."

"Sure thing. What is it?"

"I'm thinking that we could be an employment agent for security workers. We could do interviews and background checks for businesses that need security workers."

"Actually, that's a good idea. Do you think there's a need?"

"I think so. We can do a little research on it in the mean time."

We finished dinner and loaded up the dishwasher. Argus was restless, so we harnessed him up for a walk, and I gave Tim a tour of the Westmount section of Montreal.

Chapter 6

Sunday morning was quiet as I got up to make coffee. Tim was still asleep so I took Argus outside and let him sniff around, and then we came back inside. I poured a cup of coffee, and sat out on the front steps with Argus. There was a gentle fog that had rolled into Westmount from the river, but there was also a bright spot in the sky that held the promised of a sunny day.

Despite all the churches in Montreal I wasn't seeing many people heading off to services. I guess secularism had hit even this northern city. My neighbors waved to me as they passed by walking their dogs. Now that Tim was here, it felt good to be in a different city for an extended stay.

"Is there a breakfast place around here?" Tim asked as he joined me on the steps with his coffee. I must have been daydreaming because I hadn't heard him open the front door.

"There are several places in the next block." Tim wasn't under any illusion that I'd be making breakfast. I like to cook, but my cooking breakfast happens about as often as pigs fly.

"What are we going to do today?"

"I thought we'd get in the car and I'll give you the grand tour. Later in the week we can go back and see everything up close."

"Sounds like a solid plan. Now let's go get some breakfast."

****

44

The day was warm and sunny and we drove to the botanical gardens. I wasn't too sure if there would be much in bloom in April, but I was pleasantly surprised. Tulips and daffodils made a colorful carpet and it seemed that it was finally spring in Montreal. We weren't the only ones enjoying the day. It seemed like the whole population of Quebec had converged on this pleasant spot.

I led Tim through the greenhouses where most of the flowers were this early in the season. The warmth and the smell were a tonic for those of us who were weary of winter. My favorite spot was the Chinese garden and I was sure Tim would like it too.

"So what do you think so far?"

"This is great," answered Tim, "even with all the people."

"Look at that guy over there. He's rushing the summer just a bit." We were looking at a young guy in his twenties. He was wearing a tank top and shorts and it was clear that he wasn't wearing any underwear. "Hey, Tim, you don't have to take so long looking."

"Doesn't cost anything to look," he replied.

"Must be nice to be young," I said and then it hit me! I picked up my phone and dialed Hugh Cartier.

"What are you doing?" asked Tim.

"You wanted to meet Hugh Cartier, so I'm arranging a meeting," I said. The call went to voice mail and I left a message.

45

Hugh was waiting for us as we entered the small bar near the Olympic Complex. We took a table in the corner. I introduced Tim and the two of them seemed to take a minute and check each other out.

"What is the important detail you just realized?" asked Hugh.

"Is Chef Dube still being held?" I asked.

"Yes, but if we don't have more evidence soon, I'll have to let him go."

"You better let him out," I said. "He didn't do it." Tim looked at me like I was losing my mind.

"Chef Dube was seen jogging on Mt. Royal about the time Chef Boisvert was murdered. You and friends were the ones who saw him," Hugh reminded me.

"We did see him, but we didn't see a knife."

"He was hiding it. He wouldn't be running along the road waving a knife, now would he?"

"That's just it. I realized today when I saw a guy at the Botanical Gardens that there was no place to hide his knife. The knife was too large to conceal."

"What are you talking about?" Hugh looked confused, but Tim caught on to what I was saying.

"We did see Chef Dube on Mt. Royal. He was wearing a tank top and jogging shorts. It was clear that we could see his junk flapping around because his shorts were tight, and I can tell you from experience that there was no place to hide a knife."

"But we found the knife in his locker," replied Hugh, but it was clear that he was considering other alternatives.

"And was the locker locked?"

"No, it wasn't."

"And could someone else have placed it there?"

"I guess so."

"Finger prints?"

"No."

"Blood spatter on his clothes?"

"No."

"Could Chef Dube have been framed?"

"Yes."

"Then you have to let him go," I said. "He didn't do it.

"If I were you," said Tim directly to Hugh, "I'd trust Jesse's intuition. I'm not saying he's psychic, but I can tell you from experience that he can be really scary."

"I'm beginning to see that. I'm buying the next round."

I was correct in thinking that Hugh and Tim would hit it off. We were at the bar for another two hours while the two of them swapped police stories. I'm not saying I was bored, but if I'd had a gun the conversation would have ended much sooner. Finally Hugh's phone rang and he got up to leave.

"Sorry, I've got to go. That was my son and I'm supposed to pick him up."

47

"Well that was interesting," said Tim after Hugh left.

"I knew you'd like him."

"That's not the interesting part. It's you he likes."

"What do you mean?"

"Just what I said. I've watched the way he looks at you and his interest is more than professional."

"Don't be silly," I replied. "Hugh Cartier is a good-looking policeman in a city with literally thousands of great looking people. Besides he's divorced so most likely he's straight. And even if he's not I'm just a middle aged guy who even on the best day has only average looks." At one dark period in my early thirties, I removed all the mirrors in my house so I wouldn't have to see myself. Now looking back at the few photos taken of me then, I realized I was being way too critical.

"Hugh Cartier is about as straight as we are and you have no idea how good looking you are, and it's not just your looks, there's something about you that defies logic."

"That's sweet of you to say, but I've got a mirror. Anyway I'm hungry. I'll buy you dinner."

"I accept," answered Tim smiling and shaking his head.

****

Classes resumed on Monday morning and Chef Dube was there to greet us. After I talked to Hugh Cartier, he interviewed Maxwell and Jenny and

Jenny confirmed my observation that Chef Dube had no place to hide a gun, but Maxwell said he wasn't too sure. Chef Dube took me aside to thank me.

"I can't tell you how grateful I am to you," he said.

"It was just luck that we happened to be on Mt. Royal when you went jogging by.

"I try to jog every day."

"How many people know that you jog on Mt. Royal?"

"I don't know. I've never thought about it. That policeman asked me if there was anyone who might want to frame me for the murder, but honestly I can't think of anyone."

"I believe that you had nothing to do with the murder, and I'll do anything I can to help you clear your name. But I'm afraid you're not out of the woods yet. The police think you could have hidden the knife and gone back for it later,"

"But I didn't!"

"And there's no evidence that you did. But to clear your name we have to find out who framed you." And that, I thought to myself, if not going to be easy.

"I'll need your help," I said aloud. "I need to get into the office areas without being interrupted.

"Why?"

"It's best if you don't know."

"I'll call a lunch meeting with the staff and we'll meet in the school's dining room. Will that give you enough time?"

"More than enough"

****

The day's class was easy. Chef Dube introduced us to some new side dishes and we all took notes and came away with recipes. I was anxious to try out the orange beets and couldn't wait to get into the kitchen lab. As soon as class ended Chef Dube called a staff meeting in the dining room. I waited until I thought all the students had left, and then I went into the office.

Belinda Watkins and Candice Boisvert each had a computer. I carefully looked for the keyboard cables, unhooked the cable, and placed a small device in the USB port of each computer. The device would allow me to hack into the computers from a remote location. Again I wasn't sure of Canadian law, but I suspected this wasn't strictly legal. Oh well! Neither was copying files from Ms. Watkins' computer, but Hugh Cartier hadn't thrown me in jail yet.

Next I entered into the security office and placed another device on Armand LeBlanc's computer, though I wasn't sure how much security tasks he did on his computer. I knew that later I'd have to sneak back in and remove the devices since they were expensive and hard to come by.

I looked at my watch. It was time to go. Just as I was about to leave I ran into Maxwell Branch.

"What are you still doing here?" he asked.

"Just researching some recipes," I answered. "What are you doing here?"

"I left my notebook in the classroom and came back to get it.

"Want to go for a drink?" I asked.

"Sure, why not?"

Chapter 7

My head was spinning. French class was turning out to be much harder that I suspected. I was okay in class, but as soon as I tried to use French outside the classroom, I was stumped. I had a pretty good vocabulary, but trying to put together a grammatically correct sentence was proving to be problematic. I was getting better at recognizing verbs, but had no clue about verb tense.

"Do you actually understand what you're reading?" asked Tim as I sat at the table with *La Presse*, the French newspaper.

"Sort of," I said tentatively. "At least there are a lot of cognate words shared by English and French."

"You're not going to give me the lecture on the effects of Norman French on Middle English are you?"

"I will if you don't behave," I threatened. Just then my cell phone rang. It was Hugh Cartier.

"Okay if I swing by?" he asked.

"Sure, what's up?"

"Just some new developments."

"See you in a few."

"I suppose that was Lieutenant Cartier?" said Tim.

"He said he had some new developments."

"And he couldn't tell you over the phone?"

"I guess not."

"And it doesn't seem strange to you that you, a civilian and a foreigner to boot, is helping the police?"

"I'm a police informant working on the inside."

"Sure you are," he replied laughing.

Tim answered the door and led Hugh into the kitchen.

"I see you're practicing your French," he said to me as I put the paper down.

"*Oui*," I responded. "Would you like some coffee?" I asked.

"*Oui, Merci.*" There seemed to be some electricity in the air that I couldn't quit put my finger on.

"So what are the new developments?" I asked as I poured a cup of coffee for Hugh and refilled Tim's cup as well.

"It seems Candice Boisvert had a motive. She gets the husband's share of the business."

"Is the business profitable?" asked Tim.

"We have someone checking the books now."

"I'd be surprised if it was," I added. "There's a large staff and a small number of students, and the tuition isn't outrageous. And I can't believe that catering brings in any money, as catering gigs aren't that frequent from what I can tell."

"There's more," added Hugh. "It seems that Chef Boisvert had a large insurance policy."

"Who took out the policy?" asked Tim.

"He did."

"Then it will be hard to accuse the wife of anything in either case," replied Tim between sips of coffee.

"That's why I need you, Jesse, to snoop around some more."

"I've already got that covered."

"Good, what's your plan?"

"It's best if you don't know." Hugh looked at Tim for confirmation. Tim looked heavenward and shrugged his shoulders.

"I see," replied Hugh.

"More coffee?" I offered smiling.

****

I was late for cooking class and as a result I got the least popular work station. It was in the back of the class and had an electric cook top. Maxwell Branch was one side of me and Jeff Taylor was on the other side. Since Jeff had gone to school with Robert Dube, I thought I'd try to get some background.

"What town in New Brunswick are you from?" I asked.

"St. Stephen."

"Really? That's right across the river from Calais, Maine.

"And that's about the only thing we're known for."

"You must be relieved that your friend Chef Dube is out of jail."

"I never said we were friends. I said we went to school together."

"I see," I said. I didn't see at all. Why would he be taking a cooking class from someone he grew up with if they weren't friends? I made a note to check further.

"Hey Jesse," Maxwell interrupted my thoughts. "How about lunch? Jenny and I want to meet Tim."

"I'll give him a call," I said.

****

Jenny and Maxwell had no idea that I was working a case and so our conversation revolved around Jenny Harris's family restaurant and Maxwell Branch's bed and breakfast. I could tell that Tim was bored but polite. Not that their lives were boring, but Tim and I have a much more exciting life, if I do say so myself. I would have been happy to share some of our detective adventures with them, but they were pretty much self-involved today. If my life were as boring as theirs seemed to be, I might have been tempted to run through the streets naked just to liven it up a bit.

Finally the conversation moved to the murder.

"I think the wife did it," declared Jenny.

"Why is that?" I asked.

"She wasn't wearing a wedding ring when we first introduced to everyone."

55

"I never noticed that," I said. "Wedding rings aren't good if you're working with dough. Maybe she doesn't wear it to work."

"She doesn't work with dough," added Maxwell. "In fact I don't know what she really does, other than hang out in the office and terrorize the help."

"She terrorizes the help?" asked Tim.

"I've seen her have a verbal war with the secretary and the security guy. She's almost as unpleasant as Chef Boisvert was."

"So who appeared to be the aggressor?" I asked.

"Now that you say it, I think it was Belinda Watkins. She seemed to be on the offense."

"Interesting," observed Tim.

"There's more going on here than appears on the surface," I said. Sometimes I can really grasp the obvious!

****

I was sitting in the kitchen with my laptop open. I had successfully hacked into the school's computers, thanks in large part to the modern micro chip devices I had slipped onto their keyboard cords. I was reading emails and didn't find anything interesting. Most of the correspondence was business related. If they had personal web-based accounts I wouldn't be able to hack into those so easily. But the devices would keep a log of all the keystrokes entered, so I would have a copy of anything they typed. It was a severe invasion of privacy and most likely illegal. Oh, well!

I checked the keystroke logs and didn't see anything unusual, though I did note with amusement that Armand LeBlanc, the security guy, like to surf porn sites in his spare time.

"Well, this is interesting." Argus was sleeping at my feet and looked up and wagged his tail when he heard my voice. I was looking at old emails on Candice Boisvert's computer. I reread them to make sure that I was getting the story correct. I picked up the phone and dialed Hugh Cartier.

Chapter 8

V*ieux Montreal*, or as it's known in English, the Old City, is one of the most charming places in North America. Some of the stone buildings date back to the seventeenth century. Lots of narrow streets and crowded buildings gave it a charm that attracts tourists from all over. Many of the restaurants in the area have outside seating with canopies and side curtains keeping out the rain and chill of early spring. Since it was neither raining nor chilly, Tim and I opted to sit outside the small café. Hugh Cartier was walking down the street and waved when he saw us.

"What are you drinking?" he asked when he sat down.

"I'm having a black russian and Tim's having an extra dry martini." The waiter came over and Hugh ordered a martini.

"How did you ever get a name like Hugh Cartier?" I asked just to engage in small talk until his drink appeared.

"My mother was Irish and my father was French, hence the Irish-French name. I grew up in Irish section, which is why English is my preferred language."

"Where is that?" asked Tim.

"It's the area around Concordia University, just east of Westmount where you guys are." Just then the waiter brought Hugh's drink. We lifted our glasses in a toast and then talked business.

"What have you found out?" Hugh asked.

"Candice Boisvert was in contact with a divorce lawyer. She was planning to leave her husband and take as much money as she could from the business."

"Well, that adds another layer to this mystery," replied Hugh. "And how did you find this out?"

"It's best if you don't know," I answered.

"Best for whom?"

"Best for me, I guess." Hugh looked at Tim and shrugged.

"Is he always like this?" Hugh asked Tim.

"You've no idea what you've gotten into. By the end of this case you're going to be looking at the universe in a whole new light."

"I'm going to the *petit garcons'* room," I said and got up to find the men's room. When I got back there seemed to be a change in atmosphere, as if they had been talking about me, but it was probably just my imagination.

"What's going on?" I asked.

"We were just raking you over the coals," said Tim and they both laughed.

"Let's order some food," I suggested. I wasn't sure I should leave them alone again.

****

The sun had warmed chilly Montreal and the bare trees were beginning to show some signs of green.

Spring in the north is painfully slow, and I really didn't notice much difference between Quebec and Maine in terms of climate.

I was sitting on the back yard steps watching Argus sniff and romp his way around the back yard. Now that Tim was here I felt at home in Montreal and didn't have those moments of homesickness that came upon me in the middle of the night. I was using social media on the computer to keep in touch with my friends back home, but I knew the time would come when that wouldn't be enough. But right now I was enjoying being in Quebec.

Despite my misgivings Hugh and Tim had hit it off. I was afraid Tim might be jealous that I was working with Hugh, but I didn't get a sense of that at all. Of course my own insecurity feared that Tim would find Hugh attractive, but I didn't get a sense of that either. In fact they were both treating me like the slow child in a family of geniuses. And okay, I admit it, I enjoyed being with two extremely good-looking men. Who wouldn't?

"What are you thinking about?" asked Tim as he came out of the house and sat down on the steps beside me.

"The Boisvert case of course," I lied.

"Why don't we do a review of the case? It always helps when you keep note cards of the investigation."

"That's a great idea," I agreed. "I'll go grab some recipe cards." I went into the kitchen, grabbed a stack of cards, and returned to the steps. Argus was still sniffing around in the yard, but then decided to sit in Tim's lap for a while.

"The first thing is that Chef Boisvert was stabbed on Mt. Royal, near a hiking trail. He was off in a wooded section, but it was still quite a public area."

"Which might mean," added Tim, "that it wasn't preplanned. A public park isn't a good place to plan a murder."

"So it might be a crime of passion? A sudden impulse?"

"Very likely, yes."

"And Robert Dube was jogging in Mount Royal Park at the time," I added.

"Yes, but no blood spatter and no knife were seen when the three of you saw him."

"And by the time we had seen him, the police had already discovered Boisvert's body."

"Yes," agreed Tim, "but none of that clears him. He could have hid the knife and changed his clothes before leaving."

"Far-fetched, though."

"True."

"The knife was found in Robert Dube's locker," I added.

"A locker which was unlocked. And why would he hide it in his locker? Why not just throw it away?"

"Someone wanted to frame him. It's the most likely scenario."

"And it had to be someone who knew where Chef Dube's locker was."

"That should narrow down the list." I had been busy filling out the index cards and had to stop for a moment. "Okay, let's start a card for each suspect."

"Robert Dube," offered Tim, "may still be guilty and either is very stupid or very clever."

"Both are unlikely," I said as I jotted his name on the card.

"Who are the other chefs?"

"There's Chef Pierre Rondeau, and Chef Sean Kelley."

"What do you know about them?"

"Not much at all. Each chef handles a different aspect of Canadian food. Rondeau covers the French food and Kelley the Anglo-Irish recipes."

"You'll need to get more information about them. Who else works there?"

"The widow, Candice Boisvert, and we know she wanted a divorce. Then there is the office manager, Belinda Watkins. We know she doesn't get along with the Candice. And there is Armand Leblanc the security officer."

"Any of the students know about the lockers?"

"I doubt it. The lockers were in the staff lounge and we'd have no reason to go in there. I can't help feeling that there's something going on in the office that isn't quite right."

"You might need to look into that," offered Tim.

"Right away," I answered.

****

The arrival of May promises to bring spring, but there was little evidence of it on the first day of the month. A warm air mass from the south ran up against a cold air mass from the north, resulting in heavy rain and chill. Argus is never happy with the rain and always gives me a look of reproach whenever I have to send him out in the yard to do his business. As soon as he's finished he runs back into the house and waits to be towel-dried and receive a "good boy" and a dog biscuit, though I think the "good boy" isn't as important to Argus as the biscuit.

Tim came into the kitchen and poured himself a cup of coffee, walked over to the window, and looked out at the rain.

"I don't suppose there's any chance of you making breakfast?"

"None at all."

"So we have to either stay in today or go out and get soaked?"

"Other than the few blocks to the Metro, we can stay out for the whole day and stay dry."

"How?"

"The underground city of course." Beneath the streets of Montreal is the largest underground complex in the world with over two hundred restaurants, seventeen hundred shops, thirty movie theaters, plus hotels, and museums. "It's Saturday, so we won't have to deal with the commuter crowd, and tourist season hasn't started yet."

"I'll get dressed."

"And bring some money. You have to go back to Maine tomorrow, and you need to go shopping for clothes before you go back."

"I'll be back in two weeks."

"And you can shop some more then, too."

The rain let up slightly and we were able to make it to the Metro station without getting too wet. We found a breakfast place near the Atwater Metro and had a leisurely breakfast before shopping. Hugh Cartier was joining us for lunch, and then Tim and I were planning a quiet evening at home.

We weren't the only ones to find the underground city on this rainy day. As the day progressed we were joined by more and more people. We found a great clothing sale at *La Baie* department store, the modern-day Hudson Bay Company. In one small section of the underground city we stumbled upon a tailor who makes suits, and I decided to splurge on a tailor-made navy blue suit. Tim wandered off while I was being measured and returned with several packages.

"What did you buy?" I asked. I didn't think Tim was much of a shopper.

"I got us each a new wallet. Yours is pretty beat up."

"Thanks, Tim. What got into you?"

"I have to go back tomorrow, and I just wanted to get you something."

By noon time we had been pretty much shopped out. We hopped on the metro and headed out to The Village section of Montreal and found the little bistro where Hugh Cartier was waiting for us. Tim and I were amazed at the number of rainbow flags that hung from every business in The Village. Men were walking down the street holding hands and there was a festive atmosphere in the air. One restaurant we passed was full of women. Two full blocks of Rue Ste. Catherine was closed to traffic and people paraded up and down the street.

"I don't think we're in Kansas anymore," remarked Tim.

"Or Maine for that matter."

"I thought you guys would like it here," said Hugh as we sat down. "Canada is much more liberal than the US."

"So it seems,' I said.

"You come here often?" I asked Hugh.

"As often as I can." Tim shot me an "I told you so" look. Just then a very attentive waiter came to our table to take our drink orders and give us a menu.

"Good service," I remarked.

"Look around, Jesse," replied Hugh. "we're not the ugliest table here by a long shot." I looked around and he was right.

"What's new on the case?" I asked.

"I'm having trouble getting background checks on the Americans at the school. Seems the US has privacy laws. I was hoping you could fill in the blanks on the other students."

"This is getting really complicated," I complained.

"We need to nail the killer and I think we're getting close. Since we released Robert Dube the real murderer must be getting uneasy."

"So what do you want Jesse to do?" asked Tim.

"See what more information you can get from your classmates."

"You sound like a broken record, but I'll see what I can do," I promised as the waiter skipped to our table to take our orders.

Chapter 9

The sun came out and the air was warm. Sunday promised to be a good day. It was unusually quiet as the citizens of Westmount seemed to be taking their time getting up. Tim was upstairs packing, and I harnessed Argus and took him out for a walk.

Argus doesn't like to see anyone packing as he's figured out over the years that packing means that someone is leaving. Several other residents were out with their dogs and Argus made a point of sniffing each of them as they came into contact on the street.

The truth was I didn't want to see Tim pack up either, and I was just as glad to be out of the house. Tim would be back in two weeks and Rhonda Shepard was due to visit in a few days, so I wasn't really worried about being alone. Not really anyway, but the truth is I didn't like to be away from Tim, especially when I was investigating a case, no matter that it wasn't really my job. And Hugh Cartier, what's up with him?

Tim had his car packed up and ready to go. I put Argus in his crate, and we went out for breakfast. I believe you should never travel hungry.

"Do you like Montreal?" I asked.

"Yes, I do. For a city it's manageable and it's unlike any city in the US."

"I think that's what I like about it. I enjoy turning on the news and it's not about all the political wing nuts that we seem to have everywhere at home."

"And they truly seem to embrace diversity. Are you going to be okay here? You've been away from home for a month."

"I've got cooking class and French class and Rhonda will be here on Tuesday, so I'll be fine. You'll be back in two weeks, and I always have Argus."

We talked some more and then it was time to say goodbye. Tim had a long drive ahead of him, and I had the rest of the day ahead of me.

I spent the rest of the morning cleaning the house, made a sandwich for lunch, and took a nap. Argus loves to nap and is happiest if I decide to nap too. I woke feeling refreshed and decided to take a walk down Rue Ste. Catherine. As always the street was crowded, as if everyone in the city was out to take advantage of the blissfully nice weather. Before long I reached the Anglican Cathedral, one of the more interesting church structures in the city.

Christ Church Cathedral sits on top of a huge underground shopping complex that is part of Montreal's underground city. The heavy stone spire has been replaced with an aluminum reproduction, but my favorite part is the gargoyle at one of the corners that looks remarkably like a pug!

The service of evensong was about to start, so I took a seat in one of the pews and read over the service program. The service was being broadcast live on Radio Ville Marie with parts in English and French. Evensong, as the name suggests, is the service of evening prayer sung by the congregations and choir. I sat back, closed my eyes, and listened to the choir and the readings, singing along at the correct congregational responses.

By the end of the service, I felt renewed and ready to face the week ahead, which promised to be busy. Heading up Rue Peel, I found a pub and ordered a black russian, which is my splurge drink. Two sips into it my cell phone rang. It was Hugh Cartier.

"Hello."

"Where are you?"

I told him.

"I'll be there shortly," and then he hung up.

I was on my second black russian when Hugh Cartier showed up.

"What are you drinking?"

I told him and he ordered one, took a sip, and nodded his head.

"Very good."

"I'm sure you didn't come here just for drink," I said.

"True. I checked out the elder hostel program and the older members of your class seem to check out so far as my imagination goes, so I'd like you to get more information about the other three members of your class."

"You realize that two of them were in the car with me when Boisvert was killed."

"Yes, but that doesn't mean that they couldn't be involved in some way. Doesn't it seem strange to you that a simple murder doesn't seem to have a simple solution?"

Just as I was about to answer Hugh's cell phone rang. He answered and I could see a change in his facial expression and heard a change in his voice. He hung up.

"Finish your drink, we're taking a ride."

"What's up?"

"They just found the body of the office manager Belinda Watkins."

****

Hugh drove with sirens and lights flashing and we arrived at a row house in the outskirts of the city. There was yellow crime tape everywhere and the sidewalk was crowded with curious onlookers. Hugh gave me an official badge that said police consultant, and I followed him into the row house. We climbed to the third floor up a narrow staircase. Thankfully they had covered the body and the crime scene investigators were labeling all the evidence in the room. I stood behind Hugh and tried to stay out of the way while still taking in the scene. A uniformed officer came up to Hugh and began to fill him in.

"It appears to be a suicide. Self inflicted gunshot wound to the head. She left a note on the computer."

"Anybody could have typed a note on the computer. No handwriting identification either," I said. They both looked at me with a "no shit Sherlock" look. I walked over to the computer and read the note. It was short and to the point:

> *I'm sorry. I killed Chef Boisvert. I was tired of his bullying and belittling me. This is the only way out. Pray for me.*

"It looks pretty straight forward to me," said the uniform.

"Her suicide answers the question of who killed Boisvert," said another officer.

"No it doesn't," I said. "It just gives us two murders instead of one."

All the police in the room stopped and looked at me as if I was out of my mind.

"What do you mean?" asked Hugh.

"What do you notice about the note?"

"It's short and to the point," answered Hugh.

"And..." I prompted.

"It's in English," said one of the uniformed officers.

"Exactly! At the school, I noticed that Belinda spoke French whenever she could, and though her English was passable, it was clear that she was a

71

francophone and much more comfortable using French. Why would she write a suicide note in English?"

"But the gun was in her hand," added one of the crime scene techs.

"And which hand is the gun in?" I asked.

"Her right hand," answered the tech.

"Don't tell me," said Hugh rolling his eyes.

"Yes, Belinda Watkins was left handed. So let's think about it shall we? Belinda Watkins was a francophone, who wrote a suicide note in a time of severe mental stress, yet she wrote it in English, and she was left-handed, but shot herself with her right hand. Does anyone see a flaw in the case?" I asked. Everyone was looking at me like I'd just been caught blowing Santa Claus.

"Start looking for evidence of murder," said Hugh to the crime scene techs.

It was late when Hugh dropped me off at the house. I could heart Argus barking when he heard my steps. I hadn't planned to be gone that long. Hugh had followed me to the door.

"I'd invite you in," I began to say, "but…"

"Thanks," said Hugh and he stepped into the house and closed and locked the door behind him.

Chapter 10

Fog had rolled off the St. Lawrence River and was covering the city, though the sun was trying to break through. Argus was walking along sniffing everything in sight and trying to lift his leg on every vertical object in his path. I wasn't sure what class was going to be like this morning, but I was sure that it would be swarming with cops and we'd all be interviewed.

Belinda Watkins time of death was estimated to be around 7:00 pm according to the neighbors who heard the shot. I had a pretty solid alibi myself as I was with Hugh drinking black russians at the time.

It was Monday morning and the city traffic was heavy and even sleepy Westmount was abuzz with activity. Argus showed no inclination to go home so we continued on our walk. Montrealers are a hardy bunch and even in the cool of the morning some of them were sitting at outside tables in the little cafes that dotted the little neighborhoods nestled at the base of Mt. Royal.

I realized I was hungry and took a seat at one of the outside tables. Argus climbed into my lap. I ordered coffee and eggs in French, and since the waiter didn't laugh at me or correct me, I must have been doing a passable job. It was a bit chilly outside, but I had a warm jacket and the hot coffee helped.

After breakfast I found a small English bookstore, picked up Argus and tucked him under my arm and entered the store. No one panicked and kicked me out so I browsed and bought two novels to read.

By the time Argus and I got back to the house it was time to leave for class. At least I knew what to expect. The murder hadn't made the news yet, so no one else in class would know what's ahead. Unless one of them was the murderer; I'd better keep my eyes open.

****

There were no police officers in sight as I walked up to the cooking school. I was fairly confident that they didn't want to scare anyone off by being present when class started. The police hadn't released any information on the death, so I was the only one who knew about Belinda's death, unless the killer was here.

Class started and today Chef Kelley was introducing us to sauces. If nothing else at least I'd get a few recipes. I sat at my desk taking notes and covertly looking around. I didn't see anyone acting unusual. I couldn't see into the office area from where I was seated, but as soon as I could, I'd excuse myself and go to the restroom. I'd have to walk by the office area on the way and check it out.

The office area was empty. The lights on Belinda's phone were blinking, and Candice Boisvert's desk was unoccupied. The door to the security office was open and I could hear a muted conversation in French, but was unable to catch any words.

I went to Belinda's desk to take a quick look and then I saw it. The devices I had planted on the office computers were gone! A quick look at Candice's computer confirmed what I already feared. Someone had discovered the key stroke devices and removed them. Crap! At least that explained why I hadn't had any information during the last few days. There was no way the devices could be traced back to me, but it would cost me some money to replace them.

I heard a noise and thought it best to get out of the office area before I was discovered. When I returned to class everyone was at their cooking stations ready to work on sauces. My head was still spinning when Candice Boisvert entered the classroom in tears.

"I have an announcement to make," she said to the class in an almost sobbing voice. "Belinda Watkins, our office manager, has passed away suddenly. I realized how disruptive these events have been to your class, so we are going to try to carry on as best we can."

There was a general buzz around the classroom, and a look at Chef Kelley told me that he was genuinely upset. My classmates looked stunned, but they hardly had any interaction with her. Just then my cell phone beeped with a text message from Hugh:

> *Don't say anything. As far as the*
> *public knows this is a sudden death*
> *treated as a suicide. Details later. –*
> *Hugh.*

We worked quietly on our sauces until the end of class. I was happy to get away from the school.

****

French grammar sucks! At least that's what I wrote in my notebook during French class. I was in the advanced beginners' class. McGill University offers French classes for new residents of Quebec. I was in the class with Anglophone Canadians who had relocated to the area and needed survival French. By law all signs in the province of Quebec are in French. English speakers have an advantage in learning French because centuries ago French speaking Normans invaded England and made French the official language of the upper class. Eventually the Anglo-Saxon language and Norman French merged into what would become English.

Across the hall was the basic beginner's class and I could see that they had a much more culturally diverse classroom. French would be more difficult for them, but they were much more motivated to learn, I think, than us Anglophones. Despite the wide use of French, English is widely spoken and there are sections of Montreal that English predominates.

I was tired of being cooped up and as soon as class got out I started out for a walk. McGill sits at the base of Mount Royal in one of the hilly sections of town. I left class and walked up the steep hill on Rue Peel to the gateway of Mount Royal Park. There is a series of wooden steps with iron railings from the base of the mountain to the top. I didn't count the steps, but I could swear it seemed like about five hundred steps to the top. As I got higher up on the mountain, I could begin to see the city stretch out in front of me. The steps were broken up at times with switchback paths. The park itself was a nice break from the city and I remembered that it was designed by Frederick Law Olmstead, who designed New York City's Central Park and Boston's green belt.

I had to stop and rest several times and was reminded that I was no longer young and had to pace myself. Finally I made it up to the chateau with its outlook over the city. I grabbed a cup of coffee from the café and sat out to take in the view. I'd have o bring Argus up here again, but I'd have to drive him up most of the way, his short legs would never make it up the steps and I'm not about to carry a twenty pound dog up a mountain, even if it's a small one.

Sitting there I began to think about Chef Boisvert and guessed that the area where his body was found must be nearby. I finished my coffee and then hiked down the path toward the *Lac des Castors*, or as it's known in English, Beaver Lake. I only had an approximate idea where the scene was, but as I wandered down the path, I came upon and small clearing near the path that still had a piece of crime tape hanging on one branch. This must be the place. I looked around and saw that it was fairly sheltered here with evergreen brush, but I could also see the road through the branches and the back of the some building.

The area wasn't easy to see, but it wasn't far from the public areas either. I couldn't imagine that anyone would plan a murder that was so close to a public area. The grim thoughts were getting to me so I walked out to the Lac des Castors and waited for a bus to take me back to Westmount.

When I got back to the house Hugh Cartier was waiting for me on the front steps.

"Hi Hugh, what's up?"

"Just thought I'd drop by and check in with you."

"You better come in." Argus was glad to see us and I took him out to the back yard and let him run around. Hugh and I sat on the back porch. "I just took a hike up Mt. Royal after French class and took a look at where Chef Boisvert was stabbed.

"That was rather a grim walk in the park wasn't it?"

"I really hiked up for the view, and then decided to check out the murder scene. I didn't realize it was as close to the road as it was."

"Yes, it sort of shows us that the murder was more an act on the spur of the moment, rather than planned out in detail," said Hugh. Argus had tired of sniffing around the yard and had jumped up in my lap.

"There's something I need to confess."

"Oh, boy," said Hugh, though I thought he was suppressing a smile.

I told him about placing the eavesdropping devices on the office computers and how someone had found a removed them.

"You realize that that action was illegal."

"Lock me up," I answered.

"Don't tempt me. I might have to handcuff you later. Are you sure they can't be traced back to you?"

"I paid cash for them, so even if someone traced them by serial number, they wouldn't know the name of the purchaser."

"Well be careful. Someone knows that the computers were being bugged. I'm not sure that it's related to the murders or not, but be careful."

"I will," I promised.

Chapter 11

R honda Shepard's car pulled up to the condo and eased into a parking spot on the street. She emerged from her car wearing a 1940's traveling suit complete with vintage luggage. Rhonda and I were best friends and we had taught together in the same New Hampshire high school for over thirty years. When she retired to the small Maine town where I grew up to open a business, I followed her there. It was the best thing the two of us had ever done.

"Do you know how freaking far this place is from Bath?" she sputtered as she climbed up the front steps. I grabbed her luggage and ushered her inside.

"Lovely to see you too," I answered. Argus had run up to her and was dancing and barking at the same time. She bent down and gave him a pat.

"I need to pee, and I mean now!" she said. I pointed her to toward the bathroom. She emerged several minutes later and removed her hat and coat and handed them to me. She took a seat in one of the easy chairs and kicked off her shoes. I noticed they were in keeping with her 1940's outfit.

"Nice shoes."

"They hurt like hell, but they look amazing," she sighed.

"How about some coffee?" I offered.

"And cake! Don't forget the cake!"

I went into the kitchen and made a pot of coffee and cut two rather large pieces of cake.

"Tim tells me," she began, "that you've managed to get involved with murder again. What is it with you?"

I gave her the run down on what was happening while we had coffee and cake.

"So you're a consultant? What are they paying you?"

"So far I've had a few free dinners and drinks."

"And what…." The doorbell rang and Argus made a beeline to the front door barking all the way. I opened the door to find Hugh Cartier standing on my front steps. Argus flung himself into Hugh's arms.

"You seemed to have made a friend," I remarked as Hugh picked up the excited dog.

"I hope more than one," laughed Hugh. He stopped when he saw Rhonda standing in the doorway giving him the once over.

"Hugh, this is my oldest friend Rhonda Shepard." He reached out and shook Rhonda's hand.

"I'm not that old," replied Rhonda. I saw her give Hugh an appraising look. I stepped back and tried to see Hugh as Rhonda saw him. He was standing there in a well-tailored gray suit, dressed left. The suit emphasized his steely gray eyes and the streaks of gray in his dark hair. Broad shoulders and slim waist and enough lines and furrows in his face to add character. I knew I'd be hearing from Rhonda as soon as we were alone.

"Jesse has told me all about you," said Hugh as he let go of her hand.

"Really, because he didn't tell me much about you." She shot me a look out of the corner of her eye. I pretended not to notice.

"I came to tell you," began Hugh, "that the key stroke devices that you 'lost' have appeared. I had some men check the trash at the school and they found them in the trash bin."

"Good. Can I have them back?"

"They seemed to have been smashed to pieces."

"Oh," I replied.

"On a brighter note, I came to invite you two to dinner at my place."

"You cook?" I asked.

"As a matter of fact I do. I had to survive after my divorce. And I was determined not to need a woman to take care of me."

"I'll bet," muttered Rhonda.

"We'd love to," I answered. "What time?"

"Come around nineteen hundred hours."

Rhonda looked at me. "That's seven p.m." I explained.

Hugh gave us a wave and left.

"You've got a lot of explaining to do," said Rhonda. "And get me a freaking gin and tonic while you do."

"That man," observed Rhonda between sips, "is serious eye candy."

"Really," I replied, "I hadn't noticed."

"Like hell you hadn't!"

"I need to remind you that the only eye candy I'm interested in is Tim Mallory."

"It's not me that needs to be reminded." I did have the good grace to blush at that.

"I'm a fifty-something retired English teacher. No one is after me that way."

"Bull shit! You're a hot looking middle-age guy who also is kind and caring and other middle age men would love to hook up with."

"Could we change the subject please? How's Jackson?" Jackson Bennett is Rhonda's live-in love interest. He's also loaded.

"He's off to visit his children on the West Coast for a few weeks, hence, I'm here visiting you. So, is this Hugh person behaving himself?" asked Rhonda, going back to the original subject.

"Let's just say that his boundaries are a little blurred. Now it might be a good idea for you to go take a nap before we go out to dinner."

****

In all the thirty-something years I had known Rhonda, I had never seen her ride a subway. She was dressed in a 1950's party dress and was giving the Metro station the once over as we waited for the blue and white train out to the Latin Quarter.

She was giving the other waiting passengers the once-over, too.

"People dress a little better here. Have you noticed?" she asked.

"Yes, they seem to have a better fashion sense. And I've noticed that they also dress for the weather." Rhonda nodded her approval. I knew now that Rhonda would love Montreal, if for no other reason than fashion and food. We took the Honoré-Beaugrand train to the Berri UQAM station and transferred to the Montmorency train and got off at the Mt. Royal stop.

I followed the directions that Hugh had given me. We walked down Rue Berri and turned onto a side street. The street was amazing. The brick row houses all had iron stairs up to the second story. Some of the buildings also had iron balconies. Many of the houses had flower boxes. Rhonda was transfixed by the sight of the urban landscape.

"This is beautiful. Like something out of Europe," she gushed. We followed the house numbers until we found Hugh's house. He had colorful window boxes and potted plants on his front stairs. We climbed up the stairs and I rang the bell.

Hugh came to the door wearing jeans and a polo shirt, covered by a white apron. On his head he wore a chef's hat. I noticed how well the shirt fit over his muscular torso.

"Nice touch!" I said as we entered.

"Thanks! Drinks? I just made a pitcher of Sangria." He led us into a nicely furnished living room with a fire place and French doors that looked out unto a backyard.

"Hugh, this is lovely," gushed Rhonda. What's up with her?

"It belonged to my grandparents. It's been in the family for years." Hugh took off the chef's hat and apron, poured us all drinks and we sat down in the living room on some very comfortable chairs.

"Any progress on the Watkins's murder?" I asked.

"There's another murder?" asked Rhonda.

"Actually it was Jesses that figured out that it was a murder first." Rhonda looked at Hugh as if he had lost his mind. Hugh gave her an account of the case and praised my skills as a detective.

"Skills my ass," sputtered Rhonda. "The man is psychic. He knows things. Or maybe psychotic is a better term. You decide."

"You're psychic?" Hugh looked at me.

"I was brought up in a spiritualist family. I've learned to trust my intuition, that's all."

"The surprises just keep on coming with you," remarked Hugh.

"You've no idea," said Rhonda and then broke out laughing."

"Careful you don't pee yourself," I said rather perturbed and then added, "again." Rhonda reached out and tried to swat me. I moved out of her way.

"Drink up," said Hugh. "Dinner's almost ready."

On the way back to Westmount, Rhonda suddenly turned to me and said, "I like Hugh. I was prepared not to, but I really liked him." We were sitting side by side on the Metro heading to the Atwater station.

"Why did you think you wouldn't like him?"

"I thought he was trying to replace Tim."

"Are you crazy?" Tim can't be replaced. And Tim actually likes Hugh."

"I know. I just had to see for myself. I think Hugh will be a good friend for you."

"He already is, except when he and Tim begin swapping police stories."

"That must suck."

"Oh, trust me. It does."

We got off the train at the Atwater station and began walking to the few blocks to the house. As we got closer I noticed that something wasn't right. It took a few moments before it sank in.

"The front door is open." I yelled and ran up the steps.

"Where's Argus?" asked Rhonda who was right behind me.

Chapter 12

Hugh Cartier and a crew of policemen were going through the house. My temporary home had been ransacked. Drawers had been opened and dumped on the floor. Cupboards were open and things were flung everywhere. Fortunately Argus was safe in his crate in the kitchen and seemed no worse for the experience.

"I really don't know what else is missing," I told Hugh. "Most of the stuff in this house belongs to the owners, and I don't know much about it. The only thing of mine missing is my laptop."

The laptop was the first thing I looked for after I rescued Argus from his crate. The fact that the TV and stereo equipment hadn't been touched was pretty much a clue that it was the laptop they were after. But they must have been looking for something else too if they had bothered to ransack the rest of the house. My laptop was easy to find as it was on the desk in the living room.

"Did you lose a lot of information?" asked Hugh.

"I have a backup." I reached in my pocket and pulled out a thumb drive.

"Does this have anything to do with the murders?" asked Rhonda.

"I don't think so. No one at the school knows where I live. The address I have in the school records is the Bath address. I never updated the records with a local address."

"Probably some local kids looking to upgrade their computer," remarked Hugh, though I could tell he really didn't believe it.

****

After the hectic evening last night, Rhonda and I were having a quiet breakfast on the back deck. She had gone out earlier and returned with breakfast sandwiches and hash browns. Argus had tired of sniffing around in the yard and was asleep under my chair. I had a full day of classes so I was going over the subway map with Rhonda and pointing out various things to see at several of the stops.

"It's a nice day, so you should definitely go to the Botanical Gardens. That will take you all morning at least. And right next door is the Olympic Complex all at the Pie IX metro stop."

"I'm sure by then I'll be ready to come back for a nap."

"Nothing wrong with that."

We finished breakfast and I put Argus in his crate. Pugs need to be crated when no one is around. Their natural curiosity and playfulness makes them susceptible to danger without supervision. Luckily pugs have a strong love of confined spaces where they feel safe. Argus loves his crate and often seeks it out himself when he needs some down time.

Rhonda and I walked the few blocks to the Metro station and prepared for our day. I was the first to get off the train. I was a little early for class, so I thought it would be a good idea to look around before everyone else got in. The classrooms and the cook stations were empty as was the office area. The security office door was open and I could see Armand LeBlanc at his desk. I decided to lay my cards on the table and knocked on his door. He looked up.

"You're a little early for class," he said and indicated a chair.

"Thanks," I said and sat down. I reached into my pocket and pulled out my business card. Armand picked it up and looked at it.

"You're a detective? Are you on the Boisvert case?"

"I seem to be," I admitted. "But I came here only to study cooking. It seems that I'm in the middle of an investigation whether I want to be or not."

"You need to help me," he said. I looked at him. "The police think I'm a suspect. They think I was having an affair with Candice."

"Have they accused you?" I asked. This was news to me.

"Not yet, but it's only a matter of time." I didn't bother to tell him I was the one who found the video of their tryst on Belinda Watkins's computer.

"How do they know you and Candace were an item?" I already knew the answer, but I thought I'd play along.

"They found a video on Belinda's computer."

"Really?" I asked innocently.

"I had no idea she had a webcam. Why would she want to do that?"

"You were diddling the boss's wife. That could be fertile grounds for blackmail."

"I can't see Belinda as a blackmailer."

"People aren't always what they seem," I said.

"Yes, I know that."

"So, I guess my next question should be did you kill Chef Boisvert?"

"I did not." I looked at him carefully and my gut reaction was to believe him.

"Where were you when he was murdered?"

"I was right here in my office."

"Can anyone verify that?"

"Not really. No one else was here." I was pretty sure that if he had killed chef Boisvert, then he would have manufactured a better alibi. "Were you having an affair with Candice Boisvert?"

"We were fooling around. It was nothing permanent or serious." They looked pretty serious in the video, but I let that go. "Will you help me?"

"I'll do what I can," I said noncommittally.

"Thanks."

My cell phone rang as I headed out of his office toward the classroom. It was Hugh.

"Just a heads up. The media will be releasing the text of Belinda Watkins's suicide note."

"But it's a fake," I protested.

"We want the killer to think his plan to blame Belinda worked. Maybe we can catch him off guard."

"Or her," I added. I hate sexism, even in crime.

"Or her, though most murders are committed by men."

"True enough," I agreed. "Okay, I should get to class. Talk to you later."

My classmates were beginning to arrive, so as soon as I saw Jenny and Maxwell I joined them at the workstations.

"What's today's topic?" I asked.

"I think the topic is going to be soup," answered Maxwell.

"Soup?"

"Yes," agreed Jenny. "I love soup."

"Not the hardest thing to make," I complained. "Though I suppose that the instructors have been distracted by all the goings on here."

"We've all been distracted," agreed Maxwell. "I'd just as soon go home, except that we wouldn't be able to get a refund."

I don't remember what else happened after that because the little voice in my head was telling me that something wasn't right. I did manage to make a delicious soup and add a new recipe to my collection. But I couldn't make the little voice shut up. I knew that as soon as I got home I'd have to make a phone call.

****

"Je n'ai parle pas francais!" I wanted to scream by the end of French class. Not because I couldn't speak French, but because it was the only sentence I could think of on short notice. The instructor was pointing out an imaginary fly and we in the class were trying to describe where in the room it was landing. I doubted very much that I would be speaking to anyone about flies or any other bugs because basic communication was more my goal. Finally class ended and I was free for the day.

The walk from McGill to Westmount isn't a short walk, but I decided to enjoy the late afternoon stroll to clear my head. It was beginning to look like spring and Montreal was beginning to celebrate the break from the long winter cold.

As I walked along I tried to make sense about what I was feeling, but I just couldn't focus on any one thing. I had come to Montreal for a change of pace and to study cooking and French. How did I get sucked into a murder investigation? And what's up with Hugh Cartier? Why do I need another good looking cop in my life? Isn't one enough? What was the universe trying to tell me?

As I walked by on the street I saw a homeless man. He had long hair and a beard and held up a sign that read "Too ugly for Prostitution." Inappropriately I burst out laughing and reached into my pocket and put some dollar coins in his cup. It was the best laugh I'd had all day.

It was time to take a break, so I found a coffee shop and grabbed a latte and found a small table in the corner where I had a nice view of the street. I pulled out my cell phone and called my cousin Monica. She picked up on the first ring.

"I had a feeling you'd call today," she said as she answered the phone. For anyone else that would be just a casual statement. For Monica there was some reason to believe that she really did have a feeling. Both Monica and I had been raised in a family of Spiritualists. Psychic pronouncements and talking to the dead were regular events. Our grandmother was a local Spiritualist leader and had taught us to rely on our intuition. As we grew up our world view changed and we no longer really believed in the hidden world. The problem was, of course, that we really didn't disbelieve in it either. Both of us had learned to follow our intuition and more times than not, it had proved the right thing to do. Whenever I had a problem I couldn't solve, Monica always helped me sort out the loose ends. Not only was Monica Ashworth Twist Goulet my cousin, but she had recently married my best friend Jason Goulet.

"I'm in over my head up here."

"Jason and I had dinner with Tim last night and he told us all about it."

"So, what's your take on all this?" I asked.

"I think it's like the tip of the iceberg. What appears to be a simple murder is all entwined and complicated."

"That's my feeling too. When are you coming up here?"

"I'll be up in two weeks. You have Rhonda now, then Tim will be up for a few days, then I'll come up. You won't be alone very much."

We chatted for a few more minutes and hung up. I was feeling better; I finished my coffee and then headed home.

Argus came running to greet me as I walked through the front door. I picked him up and went to find Rhonda.

"How was your day?" I asked, though one look at her and I could already divine the answer, and I didn't need psychic help either. Rhonda was sitting in a bathrobe with her feet up on the ottoman.

"My feet hurt. You didn't tell me how much walking I'd be doing. Not only was it a long walk from the metro station to the Botanical Gardens, but the gardens are huge!"

"So did you wear good walking shoes or did you dress for fashion?" I already knew the answer by looking at the shoes that were on the floor beside her chair."

"Asshole," she muttered.

"Well rest up because we're going out for dinner."

Rhonda had recovered enough to enjoy walking in the Old City area of Montreal. We strolled along the winding streets and finally chose a small bistro for dinner. It was cold and we were bundled up against the northern cold front that had settled into eastern Canada. The restaurant was warm and inviting and we were able to shed our heavy clothes and get a table by the roaring fireplace.

"What did you have for lunch?" I asked.

"I skipped lunch and had coffee and cake after walking the hundred miles or so through the Botanical Gardens."

"And did you enjoy the gardens."

"Yes, I did. And you were right about the Asian gardens. They are spectacular. After that I took a ride up the Olympic Tower. Nice view, but I won't be doing that again."

"Good for you. I've never gone up there because, as you know, I'm afraid of heights."

The waiter came and brought us our drinks. I had my usual black russian and Rhonda had a martini.

"Don't you miss home?" Rhonda asked unexpectedly.

"Yes, I do. I miss seeing everyone on a daily basis. But it's exciting to be here, and I talk to Tim every night on the phone. But winter was long and cold this year and I was glad to get away for a while. I'll be back home in June when the nice weather starts up."

"Have you made any friends in class?"

"Yes, I have." I went on to tell her about Jenny and Maxwell, and several of the people I've met during French class."

The waiter appeared to take our dinner order. I ordered sole almandine and Rhonda ordered maple sugar baked chicken.

"So how exactly did you get involved in the murder and how did you happen to meet up with this Hugh Cartier?"

I gave Rhonda a rundown on the finer details of the case so far. When dinner arrived we took a break from crime and enjoyed our meals. And here's a shocker, Rhonda order the chocolate cake for dessert.

"You realize, of course," I said, "that you are a cake whore."

"And you are a perfect asshole."

"No one," I added, "is perfect."

Chapter 13

The morning was sunny and cool. Rhonda had slept in, so I made a pot of coffee, filled a travel mug, harnessed up Argus and went for a walk. The morning air was crisp and clear and Mt. Royal this morning was green and inviting. We headed over toward Westmount Square and we sat on a bench near Dawson College and took in the morning. I was getting used to the rhythm of the city, and though it was different from sleepy Bath, Maine, I was enjoying my time here.

Rhonda was still not up when we returned to the house, so I left her a note and gave her some sightseeing suggestions. On the way to the cooking institute, I stopped for breakfast, picked up a paper. It felt good to be alive.

On page three I saw the story of Belinda Watkins's "suicide" and her admission that she had murdered her boss, Chef Boisvert. I had to agree with Hugh that accepting the bogus suicide note at face value might lull the real killer into a false sense of security.

"Did you hear the news?" asked Maxwell Branch when I arrived at the school. I feigned ignorance. "It was Belinda Watkins who killed Chef Boisvert."

"Really?"

"Now maybe things can get back to normal," added Jenny Harris, who had just appeared. "Let's plan lunch today."

"Sounds good to me," said Maxwell.

"How about Greek food?" I asked.

"Do you know a good restaurant?" asked Maxwell.

"I've read the reviews of one in the Latin Quarter. We could try that out," I said.

Chef Kelley was ready to start class, so we made our way to the classroom to take notes.

****

During the morning break I phoned Rhonda and suggested she meet us for lunch. I gave her directions to *Taverna Athena* and hoped she wouldn't get lost. Maxwell, Jenny, and I headed out to the metro once class was over. A short walk in the Latin Quarter took us to a scenic neighborhood with several ethnic restaurants.

The Greek restaurant was exactly what you would expect for an authentic Greek restaurant. It was family run and decorated with black and white photos of Greek ruins and street scenes of Athens. I greeted the host in my tourist Greek, and he immediately treated us like long lost friends. We had a great table with a view of the street. I ordered a bottle of *retsina*, the Greek wine with a slight taste of pine resin. Maxwell and Jenny admitted it was good despite their initial reluctance.

Rhonda was coming down the street and waved to us when she spotted us in the window. The host rushed over and seated her and I made the introductions.

"Jesse has a fondness for Greek food, if you haven't guessed that yet," Rhonda told the others.

"So it seems," said Maxwell. "He was just explaining the menu to us."

"I've never been in a Greek restaurant," said Jenny.

"Really?" I asked. "New Hampshire has lots of Greeks. Many of them own restaurants."

"That's true, but most of them own pizza places," added Rhonda.

"I guess that's right," I agreed. "How about Vermont?"

"I don't think there's a Greek restaurant in Burlington," said Maxwell.

"Maxwell runs a bed and breakfast in Vermont. And Jenny and her family are opening a café in New Hampshire," I explained to Rhonda.

"What's the name of your B and B?" asked Rhonda. Maxwell hesitated a moment. It made me realize I had never asked Maxwell about it.

"The Sugar House Inn," replied Maxwell.

"A perfect name for a Vermont Inn," remarked Rhonda. "And what about your café?"

"We're calling it the River Run Café. We're planning on opening it during the Fourth of July weekend," said Jenny.

"It's in Concord," I added.

"Jesse and I taught in Manchester for thirty years, so we know Concord quite well."

"Do you ever go back to New Hampshire?" Jenny asked.

"Never!" I answered. "We had more than enough of the political bullshit that goes on there."

"Every four years when it's election time the place becomes a political circus, complete with clowns!" chimed in Rhonda with a hint of disgust.

"Tell us how you really feel," joked Jenny.

"But I can sympathize."

The waitress came to take our orders. I ordered the *horiatiki* the Greek peasant salad, for everyone. We all ended up ordering *souvlaki*, lemon marinated pork on a stick.

"Jesse spent two summers backpacking through Greece," Rhonda informed our lunch companions.

"I wondered where he picked up the Greek," remarked Maxwell.

"It was a long time ago." I ordered another bottle of *retsina* as we enjoyed the rest of the leisurely lunch. After we finished I said goodbye to everyone and headed off to my French class at McGill.

****

French class was progressing along. We had learned a basic vocabulary and common phrases, but now we were looking at the finer parts of grammar. To my mind they can take their *passé compose* and put it where the 'sun don't shine,' but today we were looking at prepositions, which I was actually finding useful. During a lull in the class I sent a text to Rhonda to see if she wanted to meet me after class. I told her to wear walking shoes for once.

It was late afternoon when I emerged from class, and Rhonda was waiting for me on a bench outside the classroom building. There were lots of student activity going on around us and I felt out of place if for no other reason than my age.

"I'd love to be a student again," said Rhonda as I sat down on the bench beside her. "This is a beautiful campus."

"Remember how new everything was when we were young?"

"And how important everything seemed to be."

"I don't think I'd be able to afford college now," I said.

"Yes, that certainly didn't get any cheaper."

"There seems to be such a division between rich and poor these days. I don' think we gave it much thought back then."

"That's because we were all poor back then," observed Rhonda. "So where are we walking to?"

"Up there," I pointed up Rue Peel toward Mt. Royal.

"Really? Are you serious?"

"Let's go," I said and stood up.

While we were both in very good shape for our age, we weren't athletes, so we progressed slowly. We stopped at the top of every flight of stairs as we ascended the mountain. The higher up we got more of the city was revealed. It was a clear day and the view was fantastic.

"It looks so close and yet so far away," remarked Rhonda.

"That sounds like a song to me. The walk back we be easier," I said as we rested for a few minutes. After what seemed a few hundred more steps up the last stairway we came to the chateau at the viewing area, bought two cups of coffee, and sat outside and took in the view.

"We could have driven up here," accused Rhonda as she pointed toward the road.

"Now that wouldn't be the same would it? Don't you feel that you earned the view?"

"Maybe," she remarked. She was quiet for a few minutes. "You came up to look at the murder site again, didn't you?"

"Don't tell me you're psychic too?"

"I don't have to be psychic to figure that out."

"I just had a feeling I needed to look again. The little voice is telling me that I might have missed something."

"They have medications you can take for the voices," Rhonda remarked.

"It's not that type of voice," I said, rather miffed.

"I know," sighed Rhonda. "It's just that sometimes, you scare me."

"Really?"

"Oh, yes. You have a way of looking right through people sometimes. And don't give me that 'it's just that I did graduate study in adult development' shit, 'cause I'm not buying it."

"Let's go," I said. This conversation was becoming uncomfortable.

We walked along the hiking path and then took a lesser worn path that branched off to the place where David Boisvert was killed.

"This is kind of creepy," said Rhonda as she looked around at the worn area where all the investigators had left impressions and broken branches. "What are you looking for?'

"I'm not really sure." I looked around and saw a small path I hadn't noticed last time. It led toward the small building off in the distance that I noticed before. Rhonda was right behind me as we came to the road.

"Oh, good," said Rhonda. "I need a bathroom break." The building was a public restroom and Rhonda went inside.

"If we walk down the road a little bit, we'll come to a bus stop," I said when she returned.

"Did you find anything new?"

"I guess not," I sighed. "Let's go home."

Hugh Cartier was waiting for me on my fronts steps when Rhonda and I came around the corner toward the condo. This was becoming a regular event.

"What's going on?" I asked. I motioned him inside as I unlocked the door. "Any word about the break in?"

"No, nothing new there. I doubt if you'll ever see your laptop again."

"Tim will bring me a new one when he comes up. I don't want to buy one here and pay those crazy Canadian taxes."

"I don't blame you for that. But that's not why I'm here."

"Have a seat and tell me."

"I'll go make some tea," offered Rhonda and left for the kitchen.

"I just got the final analysis on the knife we found at the school."

"And?"

"It was human blood all right."

"And?"

"We know from the preliminary tests is that it's type O."

"Thirty-eight percent of the population has type O blood," I recalled.

"Well," said Hugh and sat back in the chair. "This blood sample contained a preservative." I must have looked confused because he continued. "The presence of the preservative indicated that the blood was donated to a lab and used for testing."

Chapter 14

Spring had turned cool in Montreal, and the evening showed a promise of rain. I was in the mood to cook, so I invited Hugh to stay for dinner. I was in the kitchen and I could tell from the muted voices that Rhonda was giving Hugh the third degree, though I wasn't sure about what. Argus, as usual, had taken up his place under my feet in the kitchen.

I was putting blackberry grazed ribs in the oven, along with roasted sweet potatoes. I made up a pitcher of martinis and headed back into the living room.

"What's going on?" I asked.

"Hugh was just telling me about his career."

"I'll bet," I said. Poor bastard didn't even know that he was being pumped for information by the queen of nosey. I filled everyone's glasses.

"Explain to me about the blood," I asked. I was still not sure about what the significance was.

"As I said it was type O blood. When we had it analyzed further we found that it was not David Boisvert's blood, so it couldn't be from the murder."

"So it wasn't his blood?"

"No, it was not."

"But the blood had been donated and put in storage?"

"That was what we concluded."

"Okay." I thought about it for a few minutes while we all sipped our martinis. "So whoever planted the knife in Chef Dube's locker had access to some type of laboratory?"

"That seems a reasonable conclusion."

"But we don't know that the person who obtained the blood is the same one who planted the knife?" I was getting a headache thinking about all this.

"I guess," stated Hugh.

"So," said Rhonda looking at the both of us, "you have no idea who or what any of this is about, do you?"

We both nodded.

"Detectives, my ass!" said Rhonda and laughed so hard that Argus began to bark at her.

****

Early the next morning it was gray and raining as the sun lay hidden behind a layer of thick clouds. Everything in Westmount was glistening with reflections on the rainy surface. I was helping Rhonda load her car, and I swear she was taking back twice as much as she had when she arrived.

"Did we do a little shopping?" I asked.

"Oh, yes. I found the best little vintage clothing stores and I had to buy some things."

"Yes, I see. Are you sure you want to drive back in the rain? You can stay here as long as you like"

"Jackson is coming home tomorrow, and I want to be there when he arrives. And Tim's coming up tomorrow, and I don't want to cramp your style."

I watched her drive off and for the first time I wished that I was going with her. Montreal was nice and all, but I was ready to go home. A few more weeks and classes would be done and I'd be heading home whether the murders were solved or not, because that was Hugh's problem.

Argus spent exactly twenty seconds outside doing his business and then ran inside and waited to be toweled off.

It began to rain harder and I went and found my heavy duty rain jacket and umbrella. The weather report was for continued rain, so I knew I wouldn't be spending any time outside if I could help it. I was tempted to skip cooking class, but decided not to. French class only met four days a week, so I'd have the afternoon free. I packed up my notebook and headed off to cooking class.

The rain had let up enough for me to walk to the school. It was a rather long walk, but the air was fresh from the rain and, truth be known, I actually like rain. Mt. Royal was hiding behind a layer of fog and mist and the crowds on Rue Ste. Catherine had thinned out because of the weather.

Crossing over from Westmount to the Ville Marie section of Montreal I passed several restaurants and the morning air was filled with the smell of food being prepared for the day. I stopped and picked up a cup of coffee and a muffin. Rain always makes me hungry. So does, sun, snow, and sleet for that matter.

I arrived at the school and it was still too early for class to begin. I headed toward the security office and saw that Armand Leblanc was already at his desk.

"Good morning," I said as I took a seat and looked across the desk at him.

"Good morning," he replied looking at me in a quizzical manner. "What's up?"

"I have every reason to believe that the police will be here soon for more questions, so I thought I'd give you a heads up."

"What do they want?"

"More than anything, I think they'll want to close this case. My fear is they are going to be looking for the easy answers and move on. I'd prefer they find the guilty person, and not take the easy way out." I was hoping he'd be smart enough to take the veiled threat I was hinting at.

"You think they want to pin the murder on me?"

"You were having an affair with the victim's wife."

"It was just a fling, nothing serious."

"I'm not sure the police will make that distinction. Remember they have a tape of you two doing the nasty in the office. And the knife was placed by someone who knew his or her way around the school. Do you have a medical background at all?" The question seemed to catch him by surprise.

"Medical background? No, I've taken CPR courses for my job. That's it." I was trying to find out if he could have possibly have had access to a laboratory.

"Does anyone on the staff have a medical background?"

"Not that I know of. Candice volunteers at a local free clinic, but she just works in the office from time to time."

"Free clinic?" He had my full attention now. "Tell me about the free clinic."

"It's not really free. It's the local clinic in the next block. It does treat some neighborhood people for free, but plenty of people with insurance go there too."

"Anyone from here go to the free clinic?"

"We all do. The doctors treat us well and we send food over to them, and they use us for catering when they have office event."

"Well, thanks. I should get to class now." As soon as I was out of the office I gave Hugh Cartier a call.

"Hey good looking; what's cooking?" said Hugh as he answered the phone.

"You sound like a bad 1960's TV show. I just called to give you some information I just got out of Armand LeBlanc." I told Hugh about the free clinic. "It's possible that the blood could have come from there."

"Thanks, Jesse. I'll do a follow up. You're not bad for a private dick. Speaking of dicks…"

"I've got to go; class is starting." No way was I going to let him finish that sentence.

I took my notebook and hurried to my chair in the classroom. Maxwell Branch was at the next desk and Jenny Harris was right behind me.

"I'm glad things are back to normal," said Maxwell. He looked truly relieved.

"Me, too," joined in Jenny.

Chef Sean Kelley was reviewing baking tips with us. It was more like a chemistry class because he was focused on acids and measurements, and who knew what. I'm very aware of my own weaknesses and I can truthfully admit that math and chemistry are not among my gifts.

Our assignment during lab time was to bake a cake without a recipe, relying on what we had just learned about baking chemistry. Looking at my class notes, or my lack of notes, I was pretty sure I was screwed.

I glanced around the kitchen. Everyone else was busy doing the assignment, so I just sighed and measured out some flour. I was behind Maxwell's work station and when I looked I saw him stiffen. I shifted my position enough to see what he was looking at. Through the open kitchen door I could see Hugh and Armand talking. Maxwell saw me looking too.

"I thought they had solved the murder. What is he doing here?" asked Maxwell.

"I'm sure they're just tying up loose ends. A sudden death always leaves lots of loose ends."

****

Argus and I were sitting out on the front steps when Argus heard Tim's SUV off in the distance. In a few seconds I saw Tim turn the corner and head down the street. As soon as he parked and was out of the car, I let Argus off his lease. The pug went tearing down the walkway and flew into Tim's arms. Tim came up the walk with the wiggling Argus in his arms.

"I know just how he feels," I said. Tim put Argus down and gave me a hug.

"I miss you."

"I miss you, too. Why don't you stay for a while? Jessica and Derrick can run the agency for a few weeks."

"Maybe I will."

"I've made a pot of coffee and I've got a cake that I made in class today. You can unpack the car later."

"What is it?" he asked, referring to the cake.

"I'm not sure. It was an experiment."

"That should be interesting."

"Possibly," I said. Actually the cake wasn't half bad for not having a recipe. I guess I did learn something about chemistry.

"How's your boyfriend doing?"

"Boyfriend? What are you talking about?"

"Hugh Cartier, your boyfriend." There was a twinkle in Tim's eye. I was pretty sure I was being needled.

"Hugh Cartier isn't my boyfriend. Do I detect a hint of jealousy?"

"Hugh Cartier would like to be your boyfriend."

"Do I need to remind you that I'm well over fifty and no underwear model, and besides I already have a pretty hot boyfriend."

"Jesse, you look in the mirror and all you see is your face. We see the life behind the façade, your kind heart and sense of humor, and to hell with that, you are still one hot guy, and I don't blame Hugh so hitting on you."

"Can we drop this silly conversation?" I was getting uncomfortable.

"All I'm trying to say is that I know that I'll always be number one with you, so enjoy Hugh's friendship."

"Moving on," I said to change the subject, "we still don't have a clue who killed either David Boisvert or Belinda Watkins.

"Let's take a look at what we've got so far after I unpack. Maybe you'd like to help me upstairs?"

"I'm not good with unpacking," I said. Tim was looking at me like I was the slow child in the advanced class. "Oh, I get it!"

"Yes, you will," said Tim as he followed me up the stairs.

****

I've always had the fear that despite all my certifications and college degrees that I might not be all that bright. I was afraid that if I ever had a brain scan the doctors would see a shriveled mass of gray goo and I'd be a scientific oddity: the mentally challenged man who fooled the world.

Tim and I were dressed in our sweat suits, sipping some fine California wine, and looking at the note cards once again. I was trying to make some sense out of them and it just wasn't making any sense to me.

"Let's start at the beginning and put all the notes in order," suggested Tim. "I wasn't here for any of this so we have to rely on your memory."

"Okay, David Boisvert was stabbed to death on Mt. Royal by an unknown person or persons around three in the afternoon. His body was discovered on a hiking path not far from where the attack took place."

"So he must have been alive enough to crawl out to the path for help. How far would you say he was from the path?"

"I'd say about twenty-five feet. The bushes were thick, so the area was hidden from view, even though it was nearby," I got chills just thinking about it.

"Continue," said Tim, who seemed to be lost in thought.

"Robert Dube was also on Mt. Royal at the time of the attack. He was jogging along the road.

About the time of the murder I was driving along the road from the *Lac du Castors* up to the chalet, where we stopped and had coffee. Jenny Harris and Maxwell Branch were with me."

"I'm going to assume," said Tim," that the three of you didn't decide to kill him.

"He was an asshole, but no we didn't gang up on him and kill him. So really Robert Dube was the only one we can place on Mt. Royal."

"And the police were there when you drove back down the mountain?"

"Yes, they were."

"How long were you at the chateau having coffee?"

"About half an hour, but I'm not one hundred percent sure. We were there for some time after the four o'clock church bells rang. We had taken our coffee outside on the terrace to enjoy the view of the city."

"And the police were at the crime scene when you drove back down?"

"Yes," I answered. Tim was looking like he was deep in thought. "What's going on?"

"There's one person who keeps appearing on all the note cards."

"Who?' I asked.

"Hugh Cartier!"

Chapter 15

T he evening air was scented with the smell of spring as it wafted into the living room through the open window. Argus was curled up next to Tim as he sat in the easy chair sipping the California wine.

"You think Hugh Cartier killed Chef Boisvert?"

"No, all I'm saying is that he appears to be everywhere, and we shouldn't rule him out just because he is a police officer."

"If he did do it, why would he ask me to help him?"

"What better way to keep an eye on you as a possible witness?"

I was stunned. "But what motive could he possibly have?"

"We really don't have a motive for him. All I'm saying is everyone is a suspect. So let's just move along. What else do we have?" asked Tim.

"Boisvert's wife was having an affair with the security officer Armand LeBlanc. She also inherits a pretty big life insurance policy and a chunk of interest in the cooking school."

"Who else benefits?" asked Tim.

"Robert Dube gets controlling interest in the school."

"Is the school worth much?" asked Tim.

"I don't think so. I think they all get paid well, but it doesn't turn much of a profit, I don't think."

"We should check their books, just to see. But for now let's take a break and take Argus for a walk," suggested Tim. Argus heard his name and the word "walk" and was up and jumping in circles. "Maybe it will help us to clear our heads."

We were walking along the streets of Westmount and Argus was stopping every few feet to smell something he thought was interesting. It was a warm day, but the sky was beginning to cloud up.

"What about the murder of Belinda Watkins?" asked Tim out of the blue.

"Well, it was staged to look like a suicide, which means that someone set it up to look like that."

"Do you think it's related to Boisvert's murder?" Tim asked. I looked at him. He's usually the one who takes the lead in investigations. I usually just go along for the ride.

"Someone tried to frame Robert Dube for the murder, so it's not too big a leap to think it's the same person." Argus was lifting his leg for about the one hundredth time. Nothing came out. "And someone wrote a fake suicide note to make the Watkins murder look like suicide."

"What about motive?" Tim asked.

"I think she might have been blackmailing Candice and Armand. She had a video of them fooling around in the office."

116

"You think that might be a motive for murder?"

"Not really, no. Murder seems a little extreme for the situation."

"People have been murdered for less."

"That's true," I sighed. "Let's talk about something else. This is giving me a headache."

A car rolled past us, stopped, and backed up. The dark window lowered. "Well, if it isn't the Hardy boys," said Hugh Cartier as he took off his sun glasses.

"Good to see you," said Tim. I suspected that Tim was lying.

"How about a drink later? I'll meet you at Finnegan's Pub."

"Sure," I replied. 'What time?"

"About six." Hugh drove off.

"Does this happen all the time?" Tim asked.

"It seems like it."

****

I was sitting at my desk checking email on my new laptop. No trace of the old one was found, and no one had been arrested for the break-in at the condominium. There had been several other break-ins in the Westmount area, so I was thinking that I wasn't being targeted personally. I did miss my old laptop, however. Tim had picked the new one up for me back home.

I had backed up my files, but all my bookmarks were gone and I was trying to recall all the websites I had tagged on my old computer.

"How's it going over there?" asked Tim, who was sitting in the easy chair reading a book, Argus was curled up in his lap.

"This is a much better laptop than my old one, thanks."

"Try not to get this one stolen," said Tim as he went back to reading.

The new web browser on the laptop came with a different search engine. I thought I'd try it out and because it was called "People Finder" I decided to do some name searches. When I put my name in the search engine came up with four Jesse Ashworths. I was pleased to see that I was the top of the search with links to my two cookbooks *White Trash Cooking* and *The Stew Pot*. My name also was linked to the Bigg-Boyce Security Agency. I put Tim's name in and came up with similar results.

"Hey Tim, there's all types of information about you on the web." I told him about the "People Finder" search engine and how it claims to search on-line data bases.

"What's it say?"

"It says you're six foot four, blue eyes, dark hair and that you have a huge...'

"Very funny! So put in some names from the murder case," he said.

I spent the next two hours going down the list of names in the cases and reading the results. Most of the names had very little information about them and nothing interesting, that is until I put in David Boisvert's name.

"Hey Tim, come and look at this!" I said. Tim came over to the laptop and looked over my shoulder.

"Well I'll be damned," he said as he read the article.

****

Finnegan's Pub was a typical Irish pub tucked into a row of business on the upper end of Rue Sherbrook. What was noticeable about the pub was that English was the predominate language. I looked around and saw Hugh sitting at a table in the corner. He saw us and waved.

"I feel like I'm in Ireland," said Tim as he sat down.

"Tim's grandparents were form Cork," I explained. Hugh was wearing casual clothing and was looked relaxed and comfortable.

"The beer is really good here, as is the food. The three of us ordered beer and burgers when the waiter came around.

"Okay, I can tell that something is up," said Hugh as he took his first sip of beer. "What is it?"

I told him about playing around with the search engine. "I found something of interest about our first murder victim," I said.

"It's probably something we've already checked out," replied Hugh. "We checked out his background pretty thoroughly."

"So you know that in the nineties Boisvert was working in Lewiston, Maine?"

"We know he spent several years in the states, and that he didn't have a police record, so we assumed that his stay there was uneventful."

"I wouldn't exactly call it uneventful," added Tim.

"It seems," I said, "that David Boisvert had a bit of good luck while he was in Maine."

"What type of good luck?" Hugh looked interested all of a sudden.

"It seems that David Boisvert and his co-workers at the restaurant were in the habit of playing the Maine State Lottery every week, and that on one occasion he was the winner of close to a million dollars. My guess is that he used the money to start his cooking school."

"Good work, Jesse," Hugh had taken out his notebook and was writing down the information. "We missed that piece of news, though I doubt if it helps with the murder."

"There's a lot more to the story, Hugh."

"How did you learn this?" Hugh asked.

"There was a link to a news story when I put his name into the search engine. I almost missed it because it was way at the end of the search results and most people only check the first five or so results."

"So what's the rest of the story?"

"David Boisvert was working at a Lewiston restaurant named The Village Café, and the workers were in the habit of pooling their money and buying a group of lottery tickets. When the winning number was called, Boisvert claimed that the winning ticket was one he bought separately for himself and the winning ticket wasn't one of the group's tickets. There was an uproar from the other's claiming they were cheated, but there was no way they could prove it. Needless to say they were very unhappy. Boisvert quit the restaurant and returned to Canada."

"Which gives us another motive for murder," added Tim.

"Maybe we can contact the restaurant and get the names of the other workers and see if a familiar name pops up," Hugh said as he scribbled hi notes.

"The problem is," I replied. "that the restaurant closed shortly after that, and it's been almost fifteen years. The chances of having any records after all this time is unlikely."

"Shit!" was all Hugh said as he put his notes away.

Chapter 16

It was early morning and I was taking the unusual luxury of staying in bed. Tim had gotten up and taken Argus out and allowed me extra time to get motivated. Normally Argus gets me up around five thirty so he can eat and go out, so any chance I have of sleeping in is nonexistent. It was almost seven now, and I heard Tim unlock the front door and return with Argus in tow. I quickly put on my sweat suit and entered the living room.

"How was your walk?"

"The more I'm here the more I like Montreal. I can see why you like it."

"It is pretty great for a city, isn't it?"

"You have time for breakfast before you go off to class?"

"I don't have to be there for another two hours, so yes, let's go get some breakfast."

For some reason Canadians seem more serious about breakfast than Americans and there was no shortage of places serving breakfast. We walked from Westmount into Ville Marie and stopped at Eggspectation, which always serves a nice breakfast.

"Don't forget we're having lunch with Maxwell and Jenny," I reminded Tim.

"I'll bet we'll see Hugh again before the day is out, too."

"He does seem to show up often," I agreed. "The eggs benedict are great."

"Trying to change the subject are we?"

"Very insightful mister detective."

"Thanks."

"Tim, I tired of Montreal and tired of cooking school, and very tired of murder. I want to go home."

"Okay with me. We'll go back to the condo, pack our bags, and be on our way if that's what you really want. But it's not like you to be a quitter."

"I know. It's only for a few more weeks and I guess I can stick it out; it's just that... I guess I don't know why."

"Well then let me tell you," said Tim looking at me intently. "You like to live a very ordered, simple life. For all its familiarity Canada is still a foreign country with a different culture. And you've been working hard taking cooking classes and French lessons, and then you're surrounded by murder. Add to that the fact that you miss your friends, and you want to go home? Who wouldn't?"

I felt a little better after Tim's pep talk and headed off to class.

****

Chef Rondeau was lecturing in his heavy French accent about the virtues of choosing the correct knife and the proper use of said knives. I was wishing I had a knife and I was thinking of various ways I could shut him up with a meat cleaver.

Jenny Harris was furiously taking notes, but Maxwell Branch was rolling his eyes as if he were bored out of him mind. Since I wasn't planning on being a professional chef, I didn't give a shit about proper knives and such.

"Not planning to fillet a goose?" I whispered to Maxwell.

"Very little need at a bed and breakfast," he whispered back. "Look at that little brown nose Jenny taking notes and hanging on Rondeau's every word."

I tore off a piece of paper, rolled it up, and sent it flying into Jenny's hair. She turned around and glared at me. "Kiss up!" I hissed. She smiled and gave me the figure and resumed taking notes.

The next hour we spent chopping up vegetables and putting them in a large soup pot, which was destined for a local soup kitchen when we were finished. I had the job of peeling tomatoes, which was probably Chef Rondeau's revenge for my inattention. I popped the fresh tomatoes in boiling water, fished them out, and placed them in ice water where the skins of the tomato popped off. It was so exciting I thought I might pee myself.

By the time the soup was ready it was time for lunch. Tim was to meet us at a barbecue restaurant on Rue Crescent. We were all curious about how Canadians would interpret Louisiana style ribs. Tim was just approaching the restaurant as we turned the corner. We entered together and were given a booth near the front. Maxwell was sitting across from me where a shaft of sunlight hit his hair. I noticed that his hair had no highlights, a sure sign that it was dyed. I always find it curious that men dye their hair, as I think gray adds a little character. Jenny I noticed wore no makeup. I was beginning to wonder, too, what their relationship was. They always seemed to be together and I knew they lived at the same lodging house. It really was none of my business, but then so few things are.

"So what do you two do for fun after class?" I blurted out. Tim looked at me like I had lost my mind.

"I've been going to the school and copying recipes from the library," answered Jenny. "Then sometimes I just get on the metro and do some sightseeing."

"I like to go to the casino," added Maxwell. "I've had some good runs there."

"You play the tables or the machines?" I asked him.

"I like the blackjack tables."

"Do you ever go with him?" I asked Jenny.

"No, I'm not much of a gambler."

"So tell me about your new restaurant," Tim asked her.

Jenny went on to explain that she and her husband were converting an old warehouse in Concord, New Hampshire, into a restaurant with an eclectic menu with a distinctive decor. They had been searching flea markets and antique shops for unique items to decorate their restaurant. "We hope to open by the Fourth of July."

The waitress came over and I ordered the ribs, Tim ordered the pulled pork, and Jenny and Maxwell both ordered smoked brisket.

"I checked out your B and B webpage," I said to Maxwell. "It looks like a great place."

"What's it like?" asked Tim.

"It's an old Victorian on the outskirts of Burlington. It's got eight rooms with private baths," answered Maxwell.

"The webpage said you had ten rooms," I said.

"Oh, yes, well there are two more in the carriage house, making a total of ten."

"It must be a lot of work for just two people," added Tim.

"We manage," replied Maxell.

Our food arrived and we spent the next half hour eating and talking. We agreed that the barbecue was as good as any that we had tried in the states.

After lunch I said goodbye to everyone and headed out to French class. Walking up Rue Sherbrooke I was suddenly aware that it was spring. The air was warm and there were people out walking and enjoying the day. On the McGill campus the experimental vegetable gardens by the science building were clearly green and growing. I saw that some of my classmates were also out enjoying the spring air, and it seemed that we were all reluctant to exchange the fresh air for the classroom.

"Do you think the instructor would miss us if we stayed out here?" asked one of my classmates.

"I think if the five of us didn't show up, it might be noticed," I replied. We all started into class when my cell phone began to vibrate, telling me I had a text message. I checked the message and it was from Hugh Cartier. Really?

The message said he had some new information and would "drop by" later when I got out of class. Maybe he found out who broke into the condo and stole my laptop.

My French was improving slowly and it seemed easier to put a sentence together, plus my vocabulary was increasing. I was now able to read with comprehension, but I was still having trouble with verb tenses. I had to admit, though, that this class was much easier than high school French had been.

When class was over I found Hugh waiting for me outside the classroom building.

"Hi, Jess, I thought I'd give you a ride."

"What information did you find?" I asked. "Did you find who broke into the condo?" We walked up to his car and I got in. I was reminded again that this expensive car seemed to be at odds with the pay scale of a city cop.

"The only Canadian in your class, Jeff Taylor, seems to have some interesting connections."

"Yes, he and chef Dube were classmates. They're both from St. Stephen."

"There's more. It seems that Taylor lived in Montreal for a time in the nineties."

"Nothing unusual about that. It's a big city."

"Yes, but when he was living here he was living with Belinda Watkins."

I gave a low whistle. "That's very interesting, isn't it?"

"It's not only interesting," replied Hugh, "it puts him at the top of the suspect list."

"You think he killed chef Boisvert?"

"I think he killed Boisvert and more than likely killed his ex girlfriend as well."

"So who else is on the suspect list?" I asked.

"Everyone in that school, except you and your two friends. You have a pretty good alibi."

Hugh dropped me off in front of the condo in Westmount. I walked through the door and Argus came running out to greet me. There was a delicious smell coming from the kitchen. Tim was cooking dinner and he came out of the kitchen and handed me a beer.

"It's nice to have a man around the house," I said.

Chapter 17

Golden sunlight was coming in through the window and the early morning breeze carried with it the sound of birds chirping, and off in the distance I could hear the faint sounds of the city. Tim was sleeping quietly beside me, his face relaxed and smooth, looking much younger than his actual age. Argus was looking at me with one eye open and his tail wagging. I got up slowly so as not to wake Tim. Argus jumped off the bed and made a beeline for his food bowl. I flipped on the coffee pot, took Argus outside, and sat in the kitchen with the morning paper and my cup of coffee.

"Good morning sunshine," said Tim as he came into the kitchen rubbing the sleep out of his eyes.

"Good morning. Did you sleep well?"

"Very well, as a matter of fact. And yourself?"

"Not very well. I keep thinking there's something I'm just not seeing."

"Jesse, it's not really your problem. Let Hugh Cartier deal with it. He's the one getting paid."

"I know. It's just that I want to see justice done."

Tim sighed and shook his head. Then I saw his face change. "I just remembered something I meant to tell you."

"Yes?"

"It has nothing to do with this case, but do you remember last summer when we were investigating the murder case at the museum and we saw a strange car on our street, and then we found footprints in front of one of the windows?"

I thought about it for a minute. "Yes, now that you mention it. I had forgotten all about it. We were so busy on that murder case."

"I found footprints outside Eagle's Nest again."

"You think it's the same person as before?"

"Probably just some neighborhood kids, but I thought I'd tell you about it."

"I'm sure it's nothing, just be careful."

"I'm always careful," Tim replied.

"Yes," I agreed, "you are!"

The afternoon became overcast and cold with periods of heavy rain. I decided to head directly home rather than my usual rambling around. As I got off the metro and headed toward the condo I was surprised to see Hugh's car out front. I opened the door and Argus came bolting out of the living room.

"That you, Jesse?" yelled Tim.

"Who else would it be," I yelled back.

"Rough day at the office?" asked Hugh when I entered the living room. Tim and Hugh were drinking beer and watching sports on the TV.

"What are you two up to?"

"Hugh asked for my help," said Tim as he switched off the TV.

"I asked Tim to check on your fellow countrymen's background. We don't know a lot about the other members of your cooking class. Canada and the United States only share information in criminal cases. We have no way of doing a full background check on ordinary citizens of your country. Tim said he still has connections in the police department and can check the background of your elderly classmates from the Midwest."

"You think those old people are involved in murder?" I asked.

"Well, look at what we've found out so far by snooping around. Everyone seems to be involved in something. I just want to make sure we've covered everything," replied Hugh.

"Makes sense, I guess."

"I'll need to make a few calls," said Tim. "And I'll have to borrow your laptop."

"Of course," I agreed. "I'm going to make some bean and sausage soup, if you'd like to stay for dinner, Hugh."

"I'd love to stay for dinner."

Argus followed me into the kitchen and Tim turned the TV back on and the two of them watched the game.

****

131

Thank God it was Friday and I had finished my classes for the week. I returned home and found Tim in the kitchen banging out the keys on my laptop. Argus had managed to fit himself onto Tim's lap.

"You realize that keyboard is on a laptop and not on an old Underwood typewriter?"

"What do you mean?" asked Tim looking up.

"I mean take it easy on the keys."

"Sorry, I was just sort of excited by what I was finding."

"Internet porn?"

"No, asshole, I was looking up your elderly classmates."

"That's exciting?" I asked.

"That's for sure. Listen to this," replied Tim. "Mildred Peabody, aka a sweet old lady, was a well-know prostitute with quite a record."

"Yuk," I said.

"And Benny Goldberg, who must be close to ninety, served twenty years for armed robbery."

"There's more, isn't there?"

"And though it was never proven, Kendal Williams is suspected of being a mob hit man."

"You mean those Midwestern fossils are gangsters?"

"I think," said Tim, "that we should call Hugh and give him the good news."

"You think those old people are involved?" I asked.

"Possible, but unlikely. But I can't wait to give Hugh Cartier a nice big headache."

*****

Hugh Cartier was bullshit when Tim gave him the background on the old people in my cooking class. We were sitting in the living room of the condo having a nice cold beer. Argus was sleeping in Hugh's lap, snoring away.

"How the hell am I supposed to make any sense of this case?" Hugh asked in frustration.

"Follow the money," I suggested.

"I don't think this has to do with money," chimed in Tim. "There's not a lot of gain to be made by either Boisvert's death or that of Belinda Watkins. I'd look at revenge or power."

"Or love gone sour," I added.

"You two Maine boys are a big fucking help! I have a long list of suspects, no clear motive, and too many leads to follow."

"You're welcome!" I said.

"Jesse, go get your note cards and the three of us will look through them," suggested Tim.

"I guess it wouldn't hurt," agreed Hugh. He reached into his pocket and pulled out a stack of papers and placed it in front of us.

"What's this?" I asked picking them up.

"These are the official documents listing the two of you as consultants for the Montreal Police."

"Official? Cool," I said. Tim nodded. There was a modest stipend involved as well. At least it would cover expenses. I went into the bedroom and brought back the stack of cards I had been collecting. Each card had a sentence or two about the murder details and subsequent observations. I placed the cards on the coffee table in no special order.

"The best thing to do," said Tim, "is try to find some order amid the chaos." Move them around and see if anything makes sense."

I picked up a card and placed it next to another. Hugh did the same, and then Tim rearranged some other cards.

"This is a pretty good system," observed Hugh. "Is this what you use at your agency?"

"I actually got the idea of using note cards when I was teaching my students about research."

"We do use it, along with a lot of luck," replied Tim.

"And some intuition," I added.

"There is that for sure," agreed Tim.

After about twenty minutes a pattern started to emerge.

"Do you see what I see," asked Hugh.

"Yes, I do," said Tim. The pattern was clear, or at least not as confusing as before.

"It's not enough to arrest him on," I said looking at what we had.

"It's enough to bring him in for questioning," replied Hugh.

I looked down at the cards. Belinda Watkins's was killed and staged her murder to look like suicide. Jeff Taylor was an ex-boyfriend of Belinda's and Jeff went to school with Chef Dube. Chef Dube was framed for Chef Boisvert's murder, and there seemed to be no love lost between Taylor and Dube.

"Some of the pieces seem to be falling into place." I said. "Now if we had another connection, I think we could nail him."

"Jesse, on Monday morning I going to have a talk with Chef Dube about his actual relationship with Jeff Taylor and I want you there."

"Why me?" I asked.

"I'm hoping he might open up a bit more if you're there. You can be the good cop."

****

Tim and I were walking along the streets of Westmount Sunday morning with Argus. Argus, as usual, was stopping every few feet to smell something interesting on the sidewalks.

"We're missing church," I pointed out as we passed the stone Anglican Church where we heard the strains of music wafting out the open windows.

"Such a pity," said Tim. "I'm taking a sabbatical from church."

"It is pretty intense. Church politics seem to be pretty insane."

"Talk about insane, you worked for a city government for years. Nothing is more insane that small town politics."

135

"That's true enough. And you must have seen it all working for a school system."

"You said it. Speaking of insane, this whole murder investigation is pretty insane. All we have is a possible connection with three of the players in this little plot."

"At least it's a connection. And let me remind you this case is really Hugh's problem. We are only here to help."

I felt Tim stiffen beside me as we walked along. "Don't look now," he said. "But I think we are being followed."

"Followed?"

"Just turn down this street and bend down and give Argus a pat."

I waited until Argus fell behind us, and I turned and knelt down to give him a pat. I looked up to see a man in a beige jacket stop and pretend to look in a store window. "Is that him?"

"Yes, he's been following us for several blocks."

"Could be he's just out for a casual walk," I suggested.

"Nope, I've seen tails before and he's tailing us."

"Can we lose him?" I asked.

"Follow me!" said Tim.

Chapter 18

It was becoming noticeable that the days were longer and that soon summer would be making an appearance. Spring had been late coming to Montreal, but it seemed that overnight the trees leafed out and spring flowers popped out of the ground. In the north where summer is a mere three months long, Mother Nature compresses much in the limited time. There had been periods of spring-like days in April and early May, but now as Canada's Victoria Day approached in late May, it seemed we had reached a turning point.

My cousin Monica had called me on her cell phone to let me know she was approaching the city. Argus and I were sitting on the front steps waiting. Tim was in the house making up a pitcher of margaritas. It wasn't long before I saw her car come around the corner and pull up in front of the condo.

Monica stepped out of the car and Argus jumped out of my arms and rushed up to her barking in excitement. I gave Monica a hug and took her bag.

"How was the drive?"

"It's a long drive, but very pretty once you get off the highways."

"I think Tim has some margaritas ready."

"That's great, but I think I need to visit the ladies room."

"It's this way. Just remember to leave the seat up."

"Asshole," she said. I took her bag to the guest room and returned to the living room where Tim had the drinks waiting for us.

"So what trouble are you two brewing up?" she asked as she took a seat.

We gave her the nickel version of what had happened since the last time I talked to her. I included the fact that we were being followed. Monica thought for a moment.

"I'm not sensing any danger, and I don't feel that being followed is related to the murders." Monica's track record on "sensing" was almost a hundred percent accurate.

"I had the same feeling," I agreed, "that is that it's not related to the murders."

"You two scare the shit out of me," Tim said.

"And?" I prompted him.

"And I'm pretty much a believer."

"I need to go start dinner," I said.

"What are you making?" Monica asked.

"Jiggs dinner."

"Jiggs dinner?" Monica looked confused.

"Across the border, it's called New England boiled dinner."

"Wonderful," she said. "I haven't had that in years."

I was in the kitchen chopping vegetables with Monica when I heard Tim call my name. "Jesse, come out here!" Tim was at the window looking out on the street.

"What is it?" I asked.

"See that black car out there?" By this time Monica had taken a spot at the other window.

"Yes, what about it?"

"I think our tail is in that car, said Tim." I looked and saw a man who certainly looked like our guy. "I'm going to go out the back door and around the corner and see if I can sneak up on him from behind."

Monica and I watched from the window as Tim rounded the corner and proceeded to walk up the street. The stalker must have seen him in his rear view mirror because the car peeled out of the parking space and screeched up the street. One thing was for sure, he knew were onto him.

"No luck," said Tim when he returned to the condo.

"This seems like something that happens on TV shows," said Monica.

"Pretty standard stuff for us detectives," I replied. Even as I said it I knew it sounded stupid. Tim just rolled his eyes.

"Hadn't you better get back to the kitchen," suggested Tim.

"Yes," I answered. "It's the only room that's going to see action today, however."

Corned beef, cabbage, carrots, turnips, and potatoes cooked together in one pot makes New

England boiled dinner. Beets are cooked separately so as not to stain everything else. Leftovers are ground together and the beets are added and fried up as "red flannel hash." It's the ultimate Maine comfort food.

The three of us put a pretty good dent into the dinner, and after coffee and ice cream Tim excused himself to go call his daughter Jessica and get caught up on the agency's business. Tim spent several hours each day working remotely on company business.

"So what's really going on?" Monica asked me when we were alone.

"I'm supposed to be helping on this murder case, but I just don't even know where to begin looking."

"You want to try Grandmother's method?" Our grandmother believed that all things could be helped with the aid of the spirits. Neither Monica nor I really believed in spirits, but when times were tough and we had nothing to lose, we tried the old ways, and guess what? Sometimes it worked. I'm not saying that the spirits really helped us, but I think that maybe we made a connection with our subconscious and that gave us the insight to choose a direction.

"Sure," I answered. The method we had used once before consisted of two sets of pieces of paper with the names of all the suspects written down. We placed each set in front of us face down. We both concentrated and chose a piece of paper. If we both chose a note with the same name at the same time, we took that as a hint that I needed to look at that person more closely. If we kept coming up with different names, then we needed a new plan.

"Ready?" asked Monica.

"Ready!" We each turned over a piece of paper, and we each had a different name. We tried again and came up with two more names, we tried several more times.

"This isn't working," I complained.

"I think it means that your murderer isn't on your list."

"Well, that's going to make it awkward if the murder was done by an outsider."

"Maybe it was a murder for hire deal," suggested Monica.

"Well, if it was, we'll never solve the case."

"Did you notice that one name did keep coming up?"

"Yes, as a matter of fact I did." Hugh Cartier's name had appeared three times.

"Tell me about him."

I told her everything I could think of. I could see the wheels turning in her head as I talked.

"I doubt he's the killer, but there is something strange there for sure," she said. "He seems to be keeping close tabs on you for some reason."

Just then Tim came into the room. "Guess what," he said. "I gave Jessica a description of our stalker and she said a man fitting that description had been in the office asking questions about you."

"About me? Why?"

"That," said Tim, "is the thousand dollar question."

"I can't think of any reason anyone would be looking for me now."

"I read somewhere," said Tim, "that some twenty percent of the population is psychotic."

"Well, thanks, Tim. Isn't that encouraging!"

Chapter 19

Any school teacher, nurse, cop, or service worker will tell you that people and situations begin to unravel when the moon is full. And I don't care what scientific studies tell us, nut jobs and full moons go hand in hand. So it was with some sense of dread when Monica, Tim, and I were in the Old City walking near the river, and I looked up to see the perfectly round moon rise over the horizon as the sun was setting in the opposite direction.

"Full moon," I gasped.

"Just what we need," replied Tim.

"Oh, great," sighed Monica.

We were headed out for a very rare night on the town. The three of us had agreed to meet Hugh for a drink. This was the touristy part of the city and the streets were full and there seemed to be a festive air about the place, aided, no doubt, by the effects of the full moon. We found the little hole-in-the-wall called Jacques. Hugh was already waiting for us and waved us over to the table. This was the first time Monica was meeting Hugh and I was anxious to get her read on him.

"I've heard a lot about you," said Monica when she was introduced to Hugh.

"Only part of it is true." He replied. I could tell by the expression on Monica's face that she was "reading" him. She has the uncanny ability to see right through people.

143

Tim gave Hugh a rundown about us, or rather me, being tailed.

"You aren't under police surveillance, that much I know," said Hugh thoughtfully. "But I don't like it. Let me know if you're tailed again and I'll put surveillance on you."

"It's creepy," I replied.

"Creepy or not," said Tim, "I don't like it."

A band appeared on the small stage at the back of the room and began to tune their guitars. The music started and further conversation was not possible. People began to gather on the small dance floor and Hugh asked Monica to dance. I hadn't seen Monica dance since high school and had never seen Hugh dance. It was, well, interesting.

We arrived home a little after midnight, which for me was very late as I tend to be in bed by ten o'clock. A note had been slipped under the front door. In my experience, good news is never just slipped under a door. I opened it up with some foreboding.

"What is it?" asked Tim.

"It's an eviction notice," I said. "It seems that someone bought the condo."

"When do you have to be out?" asked Monica.

"A few days after the cooking class ends," I said.

"Well, it could be worse," said Tim, who didn't seem to be very upset about it.

"I was hoping we could have a week or two of just vacation time before we returned home." Monica seemed to be suppressing a smile.

"What?" I asked.

"Nothing," she answered and then harnessed up Argus and took him outside.

"Let's go to bed," suggested Tim.

"Yes, let's."

****

It was another bright sunny morning, and I was heading off to school. I was in the habit of arriving to the school well before the start of class and today was no exception. When I got there I found Hugh waiting for Robert Dube to arrive.

"You want to sit in on this conversation?" Hugh asked.

"Sure, why not? Are you going to ask him about Jeff Taylor?

"You better believe it."

We didn't have long to wait. Robert Dube was only too happy to talk to us and took us into an unused conference room.

"You grew up with Jeff Taylor?" I asked.

"No, not really. We went to the same school."

"That was in St. Stephen, New Brunswick?" asked Hugh.

"Yes."

"I get the sense," I added, "that you two don't like each other."

"Jeff hates me."

145

"Why does he hate you?" asked Hugh. Chef Dube made a loud sigh.

"Briarwood Academy is a private school in St. Stephens. We had a strict honor code at the school. Both Jeff and I were honor students. Someone reported that Jeff was cheating on an exam and turned him in. The administration never revealed who turned him in, but Jeff blamed me because we were roommates. Jeff was expelled. For several years after that I received threatening letters and phone calls."

"Did you save any of the letters?" I asked.

"Yes, I did. I was afraid he might make good on one of his threats."

"What type of threats?" asked Hugh.

"The threats were pretty general, but on each letter he drew a picture of me behind prison bars."

"Prison bars?" I asked.

"Yes, he said I'd end up in prison someday for what I did to him."

"I want you to go home and bring those letters to me," commanded Hugh.

Before classes ended for the day Hugh came into the classroom with several uniformed officers in tow. Jeff Taylor was arrested for the murder of Chef Boisvert and the attempt to frame Chef Dube. Jeff was also a person of interested in the murder of Belinda Watkins. When Jeff Taylor was taken away, Hugh stayed behind and offered to take me to lunch. Since Monica and Tim had plans for the day, I accepted.

It was a nice day so we walked the several blocks to a nearby German restaurant. The restaurant was done up to reflect a Bavarian Inn. The menu was written in Gothic script and I was finding it hard to read. I had to take out my reading glasses.

"Nice look," remarked Hugh.

"Apparently age has robbed me of my eyesight."

"Never mind," said Hugh as he took out his own reading glasses.

"I never know what to order in a German restaurant."

"You can't go wrong with the sausages. That's always safe to order."

I took his advice and ordered the sausage special. I have to say it was good.

"So, I guess you won't be needing me anymore now that the case is solved." I said to Hugh.

"Not for police work at any rate. But it doesn't mean that we can't continue to be friends."

"Yes, that would be nice."

"Maybe friends with benefits," suggested Hugh.

"What kind of benefits?" I asked. Sometimes I can be thick as a brick wall. When he listed the benefits he had in mind I must have turned bright red. "Oh," was all I could say. "I might be open to numbers one and two, but three and four are off the table and I don't even know what number five is." Fortunately Hugh's cell phone went off before I could dig myself in deeper.

"Sorry," said Hugh, "work is calling me." He threw some bills on the table and waved to me as he left.

"Full moon," I muttered to myself as I paid the bill and left for French class.

****

The evening news featured an update on the death of Belinda Watkins along with the news that there had been an arrest on the murder of David Boisvert, a chef at a prestigious Montreal culinary school. The police now believed, according to the news report, that the apparent suicide of Belinda Watkins was a possible homicide.

"Something's wrong with the whole thing," said Monica as she watched the news story. "There's more to the story than that."

"I have that feeling, too," I agreed. "My gut tells me that Jeff Taylor may be an asshole, but I don't think he's a murderer."

"You two are going to make a big deal about this aren't you?" sighed Tim.

"I'm afraid so," I said.

The phone rang and Tim picked it up. "It's for you," he said as he handed me the phone. "It's your mother." He smiled as he passed me the phone. I love my parents, but on the phone and in their recently acquired habit of emailing me, they gave the impression of being ready for the senility ward.

"Hi, Jesse," said the voice at the other end. "I'm calling to make sure you're wearing your socks."

"Wearing my socks?"

"Yes, I was just watching TV and Dr. Oz was talking about getting foot fungus from not wearing socks."

"I always wear socks."

"Well, you should you know."

"Hey, mom, guess who's here."

"Celine Dion? She's from Montreal you know."

"No, it's your niece Monica." Monica was waving me away as I handed the phone to here. "She's dying to talk with you." Monica took the phone and gave me the finger with her other hand.

"Freaking full moon," I said to Tim as I retreated into the kitchen.

Chapter 20

Argus was pulling on his leash as he led the way on our morning walk. It was one of those crystal clear mornings that make you glad to be alive. There was a slight floral scent in the air that is peculiar to springtime in the north. I stopped at a coffee shop and bought a latte and found an unoccupied table outside. Argus jumped onto my lap and sat looking around the street from the vantage point of my seat.

Argus usually is content to let me led the way on our walk, but something was up. On a normal day he would get in my lap and circle around and lie down. Today he was sitting up and looking around almost like a real guard dog.

"What's up, Argus?" I asked.

He wagged his tail and licked my face, but didn't answer me. Out of the corner of my eye I saw some type of movement, but when I looked to my left there was nothing there. Was I being followed again?

I was afraid I was letting my imagination get the best of me. I finished my coffee and we headed back toward the condo. As we rounded the corner it was then that I spotted him. I didn't see him at first because he was following me from quite a distance away, and if I hadn't been partially paranoid, I wouldn't have seen him at all.

I picked up Argus and waved down a taxi that was passing by. "Take me to the police station," I said to the driver.

The local police station was in an old building on Rue Stanton in the western part of the city. The police logo was visible on the sign that said *Service de police de la Ville de Montréal.* I stepped out of the cab and placed Argus on the ground, paid the fare, and then hesitated as I looked at the police station. Maybe that hadn't been the stalker after all. Maybe I was just some crazy guy that was being paranoid. Then I remembered that it was Tim who saw him here in Montreal. Was there a connection between being followed here and suspecting that I was being followed back home? I took a deep breath and entered the building.

"Is Hugh Cartier here?" I asked the officer at the front.

"He's in a meeting. Is this about a case?"

"Yes, it is." Sort of, I said to myself.

"He should be available in about fifteen minutes. And you are?"

"Jesse Ashworth," I answered. The officer seemed to recognize my name. The officer signaled another officer and he came over to the front desk.

"He's here to see Cartier. Why don't you take him to Cartier's office?"

After they frisked me to make sure I wasn't packing a gun in my shorts they led me over to Hugh's office, which was nothing more than a desk and two chairs in a glassed in cubicle. They didn't bother to frisk Argus, but I guessed they didn't think he was concealing a weapon. Argus made quite a stir and officers from all over the office came over to look at the pug. Argus was eating up all the attention.

"He'll be with you shortly," said the officer as he left.

I looked around. Hugh had a picture on his desk of what I assumed were his grown children, and a pile of file folders stacked off in one corner. A coffee cup completed the desk top. It looked very bleak, but I supposed that he didn't spend much time here.

I admit to having a short attention span and after five minutes I was getting antsy. I looked at the files on Hugh's desk and decided it would make interesting reading. I picked up the pile of files and flipped through them until I saw one that made me stop. I quickly looked around to make sure no one was watching me over the tops of the cubicles. I picked up the file and opened it. The name on the file was mine!

I looked around the room before I opened the file. No one seemed to be interested in me so I flipped open the file and read it. The first page contained basic information including my middle name and my real age! I never use my middle name and as far as I know it doesn't appear on any documents. I've always been somewhat vague about my actual age. When the drinking age was eighteen, I added a year or two and when the drinking age was raised to twenty-one I added a few more. When I turned thirty I dropped a few years and continued to drop a few as every decade advanced, after all who really cared?

I remember Hugh telling me that it was hard to get information about non-Canadians unless there was a crime involved. Did this mean that I was a suspect? And why did Hugh have a file on me anyway?

I flipped through the remaining pages. It listed my work history and mentioned my two published cookbooks. It noted that I had no criminal background and that I was presently licensed as a private investigator in the state of Maine. I saw Hugh enter and speak to one of the officers, who pointed to me. I slipped the file back into the pile on Hugh's desk.

"Hi, Jesse," said Hugh as he entered the cubicle. "What brings you and Argus here?"

"Argus and I were out for a morning walk and I spotted the guy who's been tailing me. I grabbed a cab and headed here, figuring that he wouldn't dare follow me to a police station. I don't mind telling you that I'm getting spooked by this whole thing."

"Damn it!" said Hugh as he slammed down his hand on the desk. "I don't like it. We've got enough to do without some idiot following you for who knows why."

"I wish I knew why."

"Is there anything you can think of that might give someone a reason to stalk you? Any case you've been involved it?"

"As far as I know, anyone who has reason to harm me is locked up in jail."

"How long are Tim and your cousin going to be here?"

"They'll be leaving next week," I answered.

"If we haven't caught the guy by then I want you to come and stay with me."

"Why?"

"So you'll be safe."

I wasn't sure how safe I'd be at Hugh's or how many benefits he planned to cash in on.

****

Maxwell, Jenny, and I were at our work stations making coconut upside down cake. The recipe seemed too easy, but when the cakes had cooled and we turned them over on the plate, I had to admit that they were pretty impressive.

"How much longer do you have French class?" asked Maxwell.

"Tomorrow our class is going to tour the city and speak only French. It's called total emersion day. We're getting a tour of the *Musée d'art Contemporain* in French, we're taking in a French history film, and then we are going to lunch and order in French. Then we'll all get our certificates."

"Sounds like fun," said Jenny.

"We'll see," I answered.

154

****

It was Saturday and the last day of French class. It seemed like my time in Montreal was coming to a close. I loved Montreal, but I missed Bath and my friends. It was nice to have Tim here with me for a while and great to have visits from Rhonda and Monica, but it wasn't the same.

Our French class met at the museum early for a private tour. We greeted each other in French and gathered for our guided tour. I think our guide had been instructed to speak simply and slowly because I actually found her French easy to follow. Several words were unfamiliar, but I was able to figure them out by context. I noticed that my classmates were following along, too, so I guessed we did learn something after all.

I like modern art, especially the works from the 1930s to the 1960s, but I didn't love some of the more experimental expressions that our guide pointed out to us. I also wasn't a museum person after Tim and I hunted for a murderer in one of Maine's leading institution. It's never a good thing to be finding bodies on museum loading docks. I was pretty sure there were no bodies here, but still I was glad when the tour ended and we moved on.

Our next stop was the Quebec Heritage Center where we watched a film about life in early Quebec. I thought the film romanticized rural Quebec life. I was willing to bet that life was harsh and desolate on the nineteenth century farms.

155

Lunch was a more upbeat occasion as we all sat at a table in typical French restaurant in *Vieux Montreal*. We conversed in French and surprised ourselves that we could formulate simple sentences and understand each other. We ordered our lunches and the waiter was very kind and forgiving of our attempts. The urge to break into English was always with us, but we managed okay.

At the end of our meal the instructor pulled out our certificates and made a short speech and then we were on our way.

When I got home Tim, Monica, and Hugh were there with Argus and had drinks ready. I gave them an account of my total emersion day. I was glad that class was over, but it reminded me that my time in Montreal was growing shorter.

****

Monday morning started out bright and sunny and just a little bit cool. Argus was prancing along like a show dog as we walked around Westmount. I found a bench in the morning sun and sat down to enjoy a few quiet minutes. Argus jumped up into my lap and looked around like he owned the place. I checked the area and didn't see anyone following me, so I was able to relax a bit.

Monica had offered to make breakfast during her visit, because unlike me, she actually likes to cook in the morning, go figure. I looked at my watch and it was time to head back to the condo.

Walking through the front door the first thing that hit me was the smell of bacon. Argus smelled it too and made a beeline to the kitchen.

"What's the weather like?" asked Tim as he passed me a cup of coffee.

"Cool and sunny. I think it's going to warm up and be nice today."

"I think I'm going to go back home today," said Monica as she dished out the eggs and placed them carefully on the plates. "Jason called last night and said he misses me, and I kind of miss the big guy too."

"Thanks for visiting," I said. "I always need your point of view."

"Be careful," she said. "I had a dream last night. It wasn't a bad dream, but it was strange."

"What was it?" I asked.

"I dreamed that someone gave you a key, and then you went and tried it on several doors. Finally you unlocked one and some guy came out and hugged you."

"Sounds like you had too many pieces of cake at bedtime," I replied.

"It doesn't make sense, I guess."

"Who knows," I answered. "Dreams are often symbolic and rarely what they portray."

Tim just shook his head and rolled his eyes at us.

"What?" I asked Tim. He just smiled and hummed the theme to the *Twilight Zone*.

Tim and I helped Monica pack up her car and watched her drive away. It was going to be a long drive back to Bath, but the weather was great and it would be a nice drive. Tim and I loaded the dishwasher and picked up around the house and then it was time to go to cooking class.

When I arrived at school Armand LeBlanc was waiting for me and waved me into his office. I took a seat.

"They arrested Jeff Taylor for David Boisvert's murder."

"I know," I said. "I was here when they arrested him."

"I guess what I'm asking is if you think he really did it."

"The police think he did it, and they have circumstantial evidence."

"I'm guessing Armand, but I have the feeling you don't think he's guilty."

"I think someone else killed him."

"Who do you think did it?"

"I think his wife Candice killed him."

"Why?"

"She's been calling me at home, following me, and showing up at places where I am. I've told her we're through, but she doesn't believe it. In fact she said 'look at all I've done for you.'"

While I didn't think that amounted to an admission of murder it was interesting. And if the truth were told, I did have doubts about the guilt of Jeff Taylor. Both Jeff and Candice were wack jobs.

"Have you told the police about Candice stalking you?"

"No, I wanted to pass it by you first."

"I'll mention it to chief investigator Cartier and see what he says."

By the time cooking class ended for the day I had a lot to think about. I walked down Rue Stanley and went into St. George's Anglican Church and sat in a pew to think. The quiet of the church was a nice contrast to the noise and business out on the street. I tried to think about who might have killed Chef Boisvert. I had the gut feeling that Jeff Taylor, even though he was a major asshole, wasn't guilty. I really didn't think that Candice Boisvert, as crazy as she is, was guilty either. The more I thought about the murder, the less sure I became about anything. Candice Boisvert might be stalking Armand LeBlanc, but that didn't mean she murdered her husband.

My thoughts turned to my own stalker. Why was I being stalked? It had started some months ago back in Bath, so I was certain it wasn't tied to this case. It was also clear that whoever was doing this had followed me to Montreal.

I hadn't been involved with anyone but Tim, I hadn't made anyone angry that I knew of, and I wasn't involved in any criminal activity. Who was following me and why?

My head began to hurt, and I looked at my watch and realized it was time to go. Heading out of the church I looked around to see if anyone was following me, but there was no one in sight.

Chapter 21

Argus was under my feet as I moved about the kitchen. To a pug, the kitchen is where food magically falls out of the sky onto the floor. I was chopping up carrots. Argus loves carrots and so I had to slice him off a piece and pretend to drop it on the floor. I was preparing a beef stew for the slow cooker before I went off to class, while Tim was catching up with the news in the Montreal paper.

"According to the newspaper," said Tim, "the police like Jeff Taylor for both murders."

"So Hugh told me," I added, "I hope they're right."

"You *hope* they're right? What does that mean?"

"I just have a feeling that something doesn't fit."

"Oh, shit."

"Excuse me?"

"The police have a suspect, and as far as they are concerned the case is closed. But you're going to keep investigating and harassing the police to check out other leads, aren't you?"

"Maybe," I said.

****

Maxwell Branch was pounding out a steak at the next work station. I was filleting a fish and removing fish bones, and Jenny Harris was glazing a ham. Each member of the class was working on a different dish and Chef Dube and Chef Kelly were making the rounds observing us and offering tips. Each dish was large and would be given to the local homeless shelter at the end of class. If I was any judge of food the homeless would eat well today.

"I've never really been to Burlington," I said to Maxwell trying to make conversation and get my mind off pulling fish bones out of a dead haddock.

"It's a nice town, though winters are a little long," said Maxwell.

"I'll bet," added Jenny, "Burlington gets much more snow than Concord."

"Maine gets a lot of snow, too," I said. "But we have the Atlantic that helps moderate the weather. Maybe Tim and I will come up to Burlington and stay at your B and B."

"Sure thing," answered Maxwell. "But we'll be closed for renovations for much of the summer."

"Isn't that your busiest time?" It seemed strange to me that a B and B would close during the summer season.

"Fall is our busiest time with all the foliage tourists. And winter for skiers."

"I suppose," I agreed. In coastal Maine summer was the busiest season, forcing local businesses to go all out for three months and then shut down for the winter season. Vacationers often complain about the high prices, but the truth is that many small businesses must make all their profits in the short summer season.

"Not many days of classes left," said Jenny to change the subject.

"Two weeks," I said. "Then it's back to Maine for me."

"I've got a ton of work to do before we open our little café," added Jenny.

"Still planning to open on the Fourth of July?" asked Maxwell.

"It's still the plan," she answered.

"What about you Jesse. What are you going to do when you get back?" asked Jenny.

"I'll go back to the Big Boys' Agency and Tim and I always have a cookout on the Fourth. The Fourth of July is a big deal back in Bath."

"I bet it's small town America," added Maxwell.

"It is that for sure."

****

Tim was packing for his return to Bath tomorrow. Someone had to go back and run the business, so I'd be on my own for the remaining two weeks. While Tim was busy I did some web surfing and checked my email. There was email from my father and Rhonda, along with an email from Monica telling me she was safely back home with Jason.

I decided to look at the web page for Maxwell's bed and breakfast again and check availability. Tim and I might like to get away for a fall weekend. The page loaded quickly, but I decided to give it a more critical look than the first time I pulled it up. When the web first became popular I decided to take a workshop on web page creation as part of my teacher recertification. All the teachers were encouraged to create a webpage for the school website. I had even learned to write in HTML code.

Maxwell's web page was simple, but nicely done. I went to the top of the browser and went to the page button to view the web page's source code. It was clear that Maxwell had created the page himself using a simple web publishing program. Nothing wrong with that and most people wouldn't notice the difference. I had created the Bigg-Boyce Agency's web page myself and it worked just fine.

I got out of the source code and viewed the main page and clicked on the reservation button to check availability. Nothing happened. I flipped back to the source code and saw the reason why. The button did not have a hyperlink to the reservations page. I'd have to tell Maxwell about it later.

Next I pulled up the web page for Jenny's restaurant in Concord. I could tell right away that it was professionally done, even though much of it was under construction. I noticed that they were taking reservations for their opening day.

Tim came into the room after he finished packing. "Hugh just called me," he said. "I invited him over for dinner."

"You actually like Hugh, don't you?"

"I have to admit that I do. It's nice to have another cop to talk to."

"New friends are always nice to have," I said. I was pretty sure he wouldn't be as enthused about the benefits part. I'd have to set some boundaries with Hugh the next time the subject came up.

Hugh arrived straight from work and Tim handed him a beer when he entered. I noticed that even though it was early evening the days were getting longer. Summer was taking her time arriving, but the creeping of the seasons was something that you couldn't miss.

"Something smells good," observed Hugh when he had taken his first sip of beer.

"It's beef burgundy. I figured this would be one of the last times I could make it before the summer heat comes."

"Montreal's summer heat isn't quite as hot as you'd think," answered Hugh with a scowl.

"Tough day? You seem a little tense," asked Tim.

"Just a routine police day." That was my cue to disappear into the kitchen. I knew from experience that now would follow a lot of police talk with Hugh and Tim. It was time to get some biscuit dough made.

The two cops were talking when they suddenly stopped. I went into the living room to see what was going on and saw both men at the window.

"Shh," said Tim and signaled me to go to the other window.

"Your mysterious friend is out there in that black car," said Hugh.

"This has to stop," said Tim.

"He knows what you two look like, but he doesn't know who I am. I'm going out the back and sneak up on him and flash my badge. I need the two of you to back me up, but stay out of sight." Hugh's hand went to his gun.

The three of us went out the back door and around the corner. Tim and I stayed out of the car's line of sight as Hugh went up to the car, flashed his badge, and pulled the subject from the driver's seat. The suspect leaned up on the car and Hugh frisked him for weapons. Hugh then handcuffed him and turned him around just as Tim and I approached the car.

To my utter surprise when the suspect saw us he burst into tears.

Night was coming on and color seemed to be draining from the scene and details around me slipped into the shadows. I tried to see the suspect's face clearly, but the visor on the hat shadowed his eyes making it difficult to see.

"I didn't want it to be like this," said the suspect.

"Who are you and why are you following us?" I asked.

"Please," relied the suspect between sobs, "you're the last person I'd ever hurt."

"You're under arrest," said Hugh.

"Please, I can explain."

"You've got thirty seconds," replied Hugh. I could tell he was losing patience.

"There's a photograph in my shirt pocket."

Hugh reached into his pocket and took out the photo. He looked at it closely. "So?"

"Give it to Mr. Mallory." Hugh passed it to Tim, who looked at it.

"Where did you get this?" asked Tim.

"My mother gave it to me."

"Jesse, you better take a look at this." Tim passed me the photo. It took me a few seconds for the images to register. I recognized a sixteen year old Tim and Jason in the background, and in the forefront of the photo was a picture of me and a girl named Jackie something. The photo was taken decades ago at a three day rock concert in upstate New York.

Jason had driven us there in his black 1950 Ford truck that had a primitive camper on the back that Jason's father had built. We were barely sixteen and this was our first outing. The highway was jammed with cars, and we had walked the last two miles into the heart of the festival. During the event we met three girls our own age and hung out together. It was a time of peace and free love, and it was back during the time when I still liked girls. What can I say?

"This doesn't explain anything," I said.

"I was adopted. When I turned twenty-one I started looking for my biological mother. It took me years to track her down," the suspect had stopped crying now. "Last year I found her. It turns out she was looking for me, too. We met and I found out I had a whole family of brothers and sisters. That's her in the picture.

"When I asked her about my father she said she really didn't know anything about him. All she had was a first name, the name of his hometown, and this photo."

"So what does that mean?" asked Hugh. He was shining a flashlight into the suspect's face.

"Jesse is my father!" the man said and burst into tears again.

For a second I suspected he was lying, but when I got up close and I looked into his eyes, I saw that they were light brown with gold flecks and circled with a green border. I had seen those eyes before and then realized that they were the same eyes I saw every morning in the mirror, and in that moment I knew that he was telling the truth. I walked up to the stranger and put my arm around him.

"It's okay," I said. We were both crying now.

Chapter 22

My life, I thought, had been carefully planned out. I always weighted the risks and consequences whenever I did anything, and in general I always played it safe. I hadn't planned for any mid-life surprises and I yet here I was in a place I never expected to be.

Tim passed me a shot of Canadian whiskey as the four of us sat in the living room. Hugh and Tim were in the easy chairs observing this strange scene. The stranger and I were seated together on the sofa. My mind seemed to be disembodied and floating above the room watching this little scene as if it was a Lifetime movie.

Hugh and Tim's eyes were fixed on the stranger, who was about forty, tall with dark hair and light brown eyes. Even I could see how much he resembled me. Argus was sitting in his lap and making nice to this guy. It's always a good sign if Argus likes someone.

"My name is Jason Campbell," began the stranger as his tale unfolded. "I grew up in Ithaca, New York. I knew I was adopted but my parents loved me and I never felt different as a child. In fact I felt lucky that my parents had chosen me.

"When I was a teenager and started to grow, I realized how different I looked from my parents. Where I was tall and dark, they were short and fair. When I turned thirty I realized that I had no family medical history, so I went looking for my biological parents. I told myself that I was only doing the search for medical reasons, but the truth was I really wanted to meet my parents and make a connection.

"I was watching TV one night and saw this guy who went around uniting families. I called his office and they agreed to help me. Two days later they called with the phone number of my mother. It seems that she was looking for me, too. I called her and she was so happy she was crying on the phone. We set up a meeting time, and I went to see her. It turns out she was living only forty miles away in upstate New York. I met her and her whole family. I have two half brothers and a sister. They were wonderful to me.

"When I asked her about my father she left the room and came back with the picture I just showed you. She said they met at a rock festival. All she knew was that his name was Jesse and that he was from Bath, Maine. I was working in Portland at the time so I thought it would be easy to find you. That was five years ago."

"Five years ago," I said, "I was living in Manchester, New Hampshire. I'd lost touch with everyone here. It's no wonder you couldn't find me."

"I searched all the records I could find in Bath, but the only Jesse I could find was an eighty-year-old chiropractor. And then," continued Jason, "just as I had given up I saw your name in the paper. You had dug up a buried body in your backyard."

"Why didn't you come to me then?" I asked.

"I wanted to know more about you before I met you. I knew you didn't even know that I existed. I sat behind you in the back of the church a few times. I went to the church's bean hole bean event. I even went to the Thanksgiving dinner the church put on. The more I saw you the more I liked you. You had friends who surrounded you and loved you, and I wanted to be part of that so much. I came so close to introducing myself, but then I became afraid."

"You were afraid of me?" I asked. The only people who were ever afraid of me were high school students who hadn't finished their assignments.

"I was afraid you would reject me or hate me for complicating your life. Finally I got up enough nerve to go and see you. I went to the Bigg-Boyce Agency. I had this silly plan that I would hire you to find my father and then have you realize that you were he, but then I learned you were here in Montreal, so I decided to come here and introduce myself. I was just getting up the nerve to do it when you caught me."

I looked over at Tim and Hugh. They seemed to be mesmerized by the scene unfolding before them. In fact they both had their mouths agape. Argus was taking it all in stride. You've got to love pugs for their approach to life.

"What do you do for work?" asked Tim. Apparently he had snapped out of his shock long enough to ask something practical.

"I'm taking a sabbatical to do independent study, but I'm a high school English teacher."

"You're what?" I asked. Did I hear correctly?

"I teach high school English, just like you did. I started long before I knew who you were, so it must have been in my DNA," Jason said smiling.

"I need some time to digest all this," I said. I saw Jason's face fall and tears well up in his eyes. I quickly took his hand. "What I'm trying to say, Jason, is that I feel like I just won the lottery and I'm not quite sure what to do with all the riches."

****

Blame it on my latent parental instincts, but I was up early making breakfast for Tim and Jason, even though I'd rather have a colonoscopy than cook in the morning. Jason had come over early from his hotel and he and Tim were sitting in the living room sipping coffee and getting to know each other. I can't fry eggs for shit, but I do make great scrambled eggs. I was taking fresh biscuits out of the oven, sautéing mushrooms, and grilling tomatoes to go with eggs and bacon. I also heated up a side of baked beans.

Hugh would be joining us in order to see Tim off. Tim was returning to Bath, and I wanted to make sure he got a good start. Hugh had called me early this morning. When he left last night he went back to the police station and did a quick search of Jason's background. Apparently Jason was exactly who he said he was. I wasn't sure whether to be angry with Hugh for butting in, or to feel relieved, but given the choice, I thought I'd go with relieved.

"I think," said Tim standing in the kitchen doorway, "that this is the first time I've ever seen you make a big breakfast."

"Don't get used to it."

Everyone's plates were clean. I was afraid that I might have made too much food, but feeding four hungry men didn't leave much room for leftovers.

Jason's had just finished telling us about teaching at Portland High School.

"I'm just glad you're not a cop," I said. "I've got enough of those in my life already." The two cops gave me a dirty look, so I flipped them the bird.

"Not in front of the kid," said Tim.

'The kid," I replied, "is only sixteen or so years younger than we are."

"So," asked Hugh, "is there someone special in your life?"

"Yes, there is."

"Who is she?" I asked.

"What makes you think it's a she?" asked Jason with a twinkle in his eye.

"I just assumed..." I faltered. Tim just shook his head.

"Who's guilty of heterosexism now?" snickered Hugh. Clearly I had some issues still to work on.

"See," began Tim, "heredity does play a part in it. My uncle Angus was one of us." I held up my hand to stop him.

"Does it matter if I'm gay?" asked Jason.

"Of course not. We always want the best for our children," I replied.

****

Tim had his car packed up and ready to go. Hugh had gone off to work. "I've got to get back to Bath," Tim said. "Someone needs to run the office, and I think you guys need some time to get to know each other."

"Jason, why don't you check out of your hotel and stay here with me; you don't have to go back yet do you?"

"No," he looked at me, "I can do my independent study anywhere. I think that would be great."

"Wait until your grandparents hear about you," I said. If they don't keel over in shock, I thought to myself.

"I have grandparents? That's great!"

"It might be a mixed blessing," I added.

Chapter 23

The morning light was shimmering through my bedroom window along with the breeze that was moving the curtains. Argus had abandoned me earlier when he heard Jason moving around in the kitchen. I grabbed my bathrobe and headed out to see what he was up to.

"Unlike you," said Jason, "I don't mind making breakfast." He slid a pile of pancakes on my plate and filled up our coffee cups."

"Food whore," I said to Argus. He was standing by Jason hoping something would drop on the floor and totaling ignoring me.

"I've fed him and taken him out already. I figured you could use some extra sleep."

"Thanks, it's been a busy few days."

"Tell me about it."

As soon as Tim got back to Bath the phone started ringing. He hadn't wasted any time in telling all our friends about Jason. Slowly, piece by piece Jason and I were getting to know each other. My parents didn't die of shock, even though they had long ago given up the dream of being grandparents. Jason had already spoken to them on the phone and had promised to fly down and visit with them as soon as we left Montreal.

"Are you sure you're ready for them?" I asked.

"The Campbells were older when they adopted me so there were no grandparents, and when I met my mother her parents were already dead." The Campbells, I had learned, died several years ago and Jason had no other family. No wonder the poor kid was desperate to find his biological parents.

"You only have a few classes left of cooking school," Jason reminded me.

"Yes, and then Tim's coming up to help me pack up the condo and get my stuff out of here."

"Yes, so he told me," and Jason was giving me a strange look I couldn't decipher.

****

I was sitting in the classroom between Jenny and Maxwell as Chef Rondeau was reviewing all the high points of the course as a sort of review. I realized that we had become good friends and that I would miss them when class was over. I planned to arrange a weekend at Maxwell's B and B and have dinner at Jenny's restaurant sometime this summer.

"As you know," said Chef Rondeau, "it's been a difficult spring for us here at the school and I want to take this time to thank you for your patience and flexibility as we tried to move beyond our tragedies. Next Wednesday is our last day of class and we will be giving out our certificates. You have successfully completed the culinary class, no small feat in itself. I'd like each of you to say a few words about you experiences here on our last day."

"I hate doing that," whispered Jenny.

"Me, too," added Maxwell.

"Suck it up guys," I whispered back. I never had a problem finding anything to say. I started to write down some notes, but all of a sudden the little voice in my head was screaming at me. Unfortunately I couldn't quite understand what it was saying.

****

Jason was out sightseeing for the afternoon, though I expected he really just needed some alone time. It had been an emotional time for both of us. I sat at the computer checking my email and doing some web browsing. I had mentioned to Maxwell about the broken link on his bed and breakfast web page, so I thought I would try it and set up a weekend for Tim and me. Apparently he hadn't had time to fix the link, so I picked up the phone and dialed the number for reservations. I listened to the message and then hung up the phone. "That's odd," I said out loud to myself.

****

"I want to hire you," said Jeff Taylor. We were sitting in the visiting room of the jail where he was being held. He had called me late yesterday and asked if I would come and see him.

"Why?" I asked. "You know I worked for the police on the murder cases."

"I also know you have a reputation for finding out the truth. I didn't kill anyone, but the police have me and they've stopped looking." I couldn't deny that and I hadn't been able to convince Hugh

177

to keep looking."I have some money saved up and I'll pay you whatever you want."

"Okay," I agreed reluctantly. "You'll have to hire the Bigg-Boyce Agency if I agree to investigate on your behalf. I can have the paperwork by this afternoon. The fee will be *gratis* as I'm not licensed to work in Canada. We will expect, however, that you will make a contribution to a battered women's shelter."

"Yes, of course. Thank you, Jesse."

"Now tell me why you are innocent and why it is that the police don't believe you."

****

"So," said Hugh as we sat over lunch the next day. "You believe that Jeff Taylor is innocent?"

"As I've said before Jeff Taylor is an asshole, but I don't think he's a murderer. It's a gut feeling, but I admit, he hasn't given me much to work with."

"The last thing I want," said Hugh, "is to send an innocent man to prison, but so far everything points to him. Unless you come up with something new, we'll have to let the court decide whether he is guilty or not."

We were having lunch in "the village" at a little bistro. The weather was warm and sunny and we were at a table outside. Hugh reached over and took my hand.

"Jesse, I'm going to miss you."

"I'll miss you too, Hugh."

"You could stay here, you know."

"No I couldn't. Canada's immigration laws are even stricter that ours in the US. I've about used up my student visa time as it is."

"You could stay with me. I can pull strings."

"My life is in a little town in Maine, three hundred something miles away."

"It's Tim you're going back to, isn't it?"

"Of course it's Tim," I said. "And I'm not dense, Hugh. I've never been a fool. I know what you've been asking me these last weeks. And my question is why? I'm a middle-aged, middle class baby boomer, and not particularly special."

"You are so wrong about that. It's the total package that's so appealing."

"Hugh, I've never believed that the human heart has limitations, that we can only love one person at a time. Nor do I believe that love is bounded by time or space, or life and death, for that matter. And whatever relationship two people have is for them alone. But the truth is that after next week I'll be leaving Montreal, and probably won't be back for a long time."

"We'll see about that," said Hugh mysteriously.

I wasn't sure I had resolved anything with Hugh or not, but I made it clear that Tim was the one and Hugh and I could be friends from a safe distance. I was going to confront him about why he had a file on me at his desk, but the time hadn't seemed right. I intended to get that cleared away, however, as soon as possible.

I was at my desk paying some bills when I came across the thumb drive that I had copied files from the school's office. I decided to take one last look before I erased the files. I opened up the folder to Candice Boisvert's files and saw nothing unusual. But then I noticed an icon called trash. I must have copied the desktop files as well as the documents file since there were also a few shortcut icons as well.

It was an email from David Boisvert's insurance company. It seems they refused to pay up until there was an arrest for the murder. I guess they weren't about to pay out to the wife until she was cleared of the crime.

A closer look at the email response she sent convinced me that Candice Boisvert was a complete sociopath, but wasn't evidence enough to make here guilty of murder. I printed out the document anyway, just in case.

I still had two phone calls to make. I needed to call the insurance company about Boisvert's policy and I needed to call the clinic and ask about the blood. I was hoping it would point to Candice as the killer of both the victims, but the little voice was telling me that would be too easy.

****

Argus was trotting along in his best show dog gait as Jason and I followed behind him. We were taking a walk in Mt. Royal Park and looking at the city skyline as we made our way along the trail. Jason and I found it easier to talk during our walks and Argus was always ready to go.

"Will you be going back to Portland High in the fall?" I asked.

"Yes, unless something else comes along. I've put in applications to some other schools as well."

"Schools far away?" I was afraid of the answer.

"No, they're all in southern Maine. I hope you don't mind, but I want to stay close to you."

"I'm glad. But what about your mother?" I asked. Truthfully I had a hard time remembering her and if it wasn't for the picture I wouldn't be able to imagine her face. The festival was decades ago, and it was all a bit unreal and hazy as it was.

"I love visiting her, but she has a family already."

"I see."

"How do you feel about that?" he asked.

"Sad that I've missed so much," I confessed. "But glad you're here now. And very grateful to the Cambells for the great job they did with you."

We walked in silence for the next quarter mile or so, watching Argus sniff his way along.

"Is it okay if I call you dad?"

"Yes," I said as tears threatened to spill down my face.

Chapter 24

The sky began to cloud up and the wind direction changed as rain threatened to pour down over the city of Montreal. One thing that the Province of Quebec and the region of New England have in common is the unpredictably of the weather.

I was sitting at my desk trying to tackle the problem of getting Jeff Taylor set free. I had my doubts about Jeff, but the little voice was telling me that he wasn't guilty of murder. The voice was telling me that I only needed one more piece of the puzzle and then I could see the solution. The truth of the matter was that the little voice was getting to be really annoying.

I knew how it really worked. My subconscious mind was constantly gathering data and trying to fit the pieces together. Once the missing piece was in place I could figure out the puzzle. At least that's how it usually worked. I wasn't sure how it was going to work today.

All murders have a motive. Jeff's motive was revenge seemed farfetched to me. He was kicked out of school, so he murdered someone in order to frame the person he suspected had turned him in to the school authorities? And then he murdered a former girlfriend and made it look like suicide? Jeff Taylor didn't strike me as that bright.

No, I was going about this all wrong. I should be looking at the murder victims rather than the suspects. I envied my grandmother. She believed she could communicate with the dead. Maybe she would have spoken with them and they would have told her who killed them. I hadn't told Jason about that part of our family history yet. I wondered if he had inherited any of the so called "gifts."

But I knew the dead were dead and wouldn't be telling me anything, and it was up to me to find the truth, to speak for them, and to give them justice. What were the motives? It would be best to look at the murder victims one at a time.

I had a good idea who might have killed Belinda Watkins, but there was no way to prove it, but maybe that would come later. Belinda had videoed a "situation" between Armand LeBlanc and Candice Boisvert. Was she blackmailing them and was it worth murdering her for?

It was David Boisvert that offered the challenge. It's always hard to find a suspect when the victim was somebody that everyone hated. Boisvert was selfish, outspoken, and a general asshole, and had more enemies than friends.

Boisvert had won a lot of money in the lottery and had used the money to set up the culinary school. Robert Dube was a co-owner of the school and would become the head of the school upon Boisvert's death. The wife, Candice, would get a major share of the school and also would collect on his life insurance policy. The problem was that the school was not a big money maker and barely broke even. The insurance policy wasn't large enough to make murder profitable, and I thought Candice would have made out as well in a divorce settlement. In fact she was planning to divorce him. No, Candice didn't kill her husband.

Jeff Taylor looked good for the murder, according to police. But the motive was too weak. If Robert Dube had been murdered, then I could see him as the killer. But to kill someone just to frame your enemy for an imagined incident that happened years ago, just didn't make sense.

"Dad, you've been staring at the computer for over an hour. Take a break." I looked up to see Jason's look of concern. "Let me take you out to dinner."

"Okay, my head is beginning to hurt anyway." I realized I was hungry. "How about we go to a nice Greek restaurant?"

"Do you have one in mind?"

"Yes, have you been to the Latin Quarter yet?"

"No, though I've heard it's nice."

"Well the rain has stopped, so let's talk a walk and have some dinner."

Jason wasn't all that well versed in Greek food, so I explained the menu as best I could. The waiter at the restaurant remembered me and greeted me in Greek, and seated us at a table near the window where we had a great view of the street.

"This section of the city really is picturesque," said Jason.

"We'll have to bring Argus with us and take a nice long walk."

"That would be great, dad."

The meal was exceptionally good and Jason loved the *stifado*. I promised to make it for him when we got back home. We ended the meal with Greek coffee and baklava. Jason turned to me.

"You remember on that first night when you found out about me, you said you felt like you won the lottery?"

"I do indeed."

"That's how I feel. I feel like I won the lottery, too."

Something in my mind clicked. A piece of the puzzle fell in place. I slammed my fist on the table. "That's it! That's the answer!"

Jason looked alarmed. "What's wrong?" he asked.

"You just helped me solve the murder. That's the answer!"

****

When David Boisvert won the lottery back in Lewiston, Maine, there were a whole lot of his coworkers who thought they had been cheated. Boisvert claimed that the winning ticket was one he bought on his own and was not one of those that he had bought on behalf of his coworkers. The lottery commission had backed up Boisvert by examining the time of the purchase of the ticket. There had been a ticket with ten numbers purchased at 10:00 am and a single ticket purchased at 10:02 am on the day of the lottery drawing. It was the single ticket number that had been the winner, but I imagine that his coworkers were unhappy with the results. The issue, as they saw it, was that he was supposed to have purchased twelve numbers for the group, not ten. The winning number, they contended, should belong to the group. Boisvert claimed that he only received ten dollars from the group, and so that is what he bought.

The news story had proved to be one of the top stories on the day and so it wasn't hard to find newspaper accounts of it on the web. I was disappointed, however, when I read the list of names of his coworkers. I expected to be able to get a clue to the case when I looked at the list of names.

If there were news stories I was sure there were probably some news photos taken at the time. It took me over an hour of searching, but I finally found a news photo in the archives of the *Bangor Daily News*. It was a picture of a news conference that Boisvert's coworkers had put on to present their case. Time, name changes, and cosmetic enhancements had changed, but as I looked at the photographs of Boisvert's coworkers, and there, plain as day, I saw what I was looking for. I knew who killed David Boisvert!

What was even worse was the sense of betrayal I felt. Not only had I been pulled into a murder investigation, but also I had unwittingly helped with the murder.

I was angry and I picked up the phone.

****

The Culinary Institute of Montreal was preparing for the graduation ceremony for its spring semester students. The day was warm and sunny and the chefs had been preparing the refreshments for the reception. Each student approached the podium and gave a little speech on how they planned to use the skills they learned at the school.

I had a very different speech planned, one that would shock the other students and hopefully would reveal a killer. Hugh Cartier sat in the back of the room pretending to be a casual observer. But beyond the classroom doors there were armed police officers ready to jump into action if needed. My biggest fear was that I would be unable to make a case for murder and just embarrass myself.

Finally, it was my turn to say a few words before we all went our separate ways. I had chosen to go last and so when it was my turn I stood in front of the class. It took me a second or two to start as I began to think that perhaps I got it all wrong and was making a complete ass of myself. I gathered up my thoughts and began.

"As most of you know by now I'm a private investigator, here to do some personal skill building. I find cooking to be my way of relaxing." Everyone was looking at me and nodding, almost as if they weren't really paying attention. My next words shocked them, and all eyes were riveted on me.

"There's nothing relaxing about murder and though it's a tragedy that two persons were murdered here at this school, it's even more tragic that someone in this room is the murderer.

"It's true that the police had a suspect in jail and thought the case was closed, but make no mistake, Jeff Taylor is not the murderer." The class members began to shift their seats and look around each other. At the back of the room, out of view of the class, four police officers stepped into the classroom.

"The first mistake was thinking that the two murders were committed by the same person. They weren't. I've long suspected that Belinda Watsons's murder had nothing to do with David Boisvert's murder. A call to the insurance company confirmed my suspicion that there would be no payout until the murder was solved. What better way to solve a murder than have a confession in writing from a supposed suicide. Don't you agree Candice?"

"You're crazy if you think I did it," said Candice. She had half risen from her seat. She looked around at the class with wild eyes. Everyone in the room was looking at her now.

"Then perhaps you can explain these emails I found in the on your computer?" I asked as I held up the printout.

"You bastard!" she yelled and made a run for the door. Two of the police officers captured her and escorted her out the door.

"That explains one of the murders," I said to the class. By now they were all looking at me in shock and disbelief. "Belinda's murder was a crime of passion and blackmail, and so Candice, I think, with the help of a good attorney, may get off with a lighter sentence. But the murder of David Boisvert was a carefully planned act of revenge, and there will be no mitigating circumstances in this case.

"In fact the plan was so intricate that it took more than one person to pull it off. And what really makes me angry is that I was used to create the perfect alibi." There was a commotion in the back of the room as someone tried to run out the back door, only to be stopped by the police.

"It seems that David Boisvert, when he was working in Lewiston, Maine, won the lottery, but his coworkers believed they had been cheated out of their share of a what they thought was a shared ticket. I suspected there might be a connection, but looking at the list of names there didn't seem to be one. It wasn't until I looked closely at a news photo of the coworkers that I recognized two familiar faces. Even though years had passed, and cosmetic changes had been made with hair color and fashion, there are certain things that can't be changed. Have you ever really taken a close look at people's ears? Take a look sometime and notice that most people had free hanging earlobes and a few people have attached earlobes. In fact ears are almost as unique as finger prints. Eye brows are another unique feature, as are cheekbones and foreheads, and noses. I could go on and on, but the point is if you look closely and pay attention you can notice things.

"I must have looked at that photo a hundred times and then finally two faces began to appear, that of Maxwell Branch, and Jenny Harris."

Hugh appeared and with the other officers; there was a scuffle in the back of the classroom and Maxwell and Jenny were taken away in handcuffs.

"The last piece of damning evidence is the fact that the police just searched their lodgings and found my laptop, Maxwell and Jenny were the only ones who knew where I lived. I should have seen that earlier." There was stunned silence in the room and then a general buzz of confusion until Armand Leblanc asked a question.

"But how did they commit murder when you were with them at the time of the murder?" he asked as soon as the room settled down.

"That took me some time to figure out too, but then I remembered the events of the day. At the beginning of the course Maxwell and Jenny sort of befriended me and we decided to go out for lunch. That was when I offered to give them a tour of the city and take them up to Mt. Royal. I remembered that Maxwell left the lunch to make a call. My guess is that he called Boisvert and set up a meeting at the hiking path of Mt. Royal. They were insistent that we be at the top of the mountain at four o'clock to hear the bells. I'm pretty sure they knew that Robert Dube was in the habit of jogging up there and would be the perfect fall guy.

"On our trip up the mountain, Jenny and Maxwell stopped to use the restroom, or so they said. I suspect that one of them, or both, slipped away long enough to kill Boisvert. And then calmly returned to the car where I was waiting."

"How is it that Boisvert didn't recognize them?" asked Armand.

"I'm not sure how closely they worked together, but in any case it had been years and people change. Jenny had short hair and was overweight then. Now she is thin and fit and has long red hair. Maxwell was blond and wore glasses. But I noticed the other day that his hair was dyed and he wears contacts. So there major physical traits had changed and Boisvert, I'm sure, never expected to see them again. I was only able to identify them in the photo because I was looking for them, otherwise they would have gone unnoticed."

"What about the blood on the knife," asked Armand. I had to hand it to him; he'd make a good investigator.

"I called the clinic and discovered that Jenny Harris had registered at the clinic to be a volunteer two weeks before class began. Clearly she had the opportunity to snag a blood sample. As I said, this was all carefully planned out."

Suddenly I felt very tired and the events of the last two days were affecting me and I felt drained. We all left the classroom and the reporters were waiting outside.

"Hey sailor," said Hugh Cartier, "can I buy you a cup of coffee?" Hugh steered me away from the media.

"Make it something stronger and you've got a deal."

****

"So you really were bluffing about Candice Boisvert being guilty of killing Belinda Watkins?" Jason asked me later that night when things had settled down..

"Yes, I hoped that if I held up the printout I found on her computer that she would freak out."

"And she did," said Hugh. "She confessed to the murder, otherwise we wouldn't have enough evidence to go forward."

"What was the printout?" asked Jason.

"Just a note telling Belinda that blackmail wasn't going to work and she could do what she wanted with the video."

"But she killed Belinda anyway?"

"Yes, the note was a bluff. Candice hoped to take the wind out of her sails, but Belinda was going to show the video to Boisvert, which meant Candice wouldn't have gotten anything out of the divorce. And Hugh, can you explain to me why you had a file on me in your office?"

"When I thought you were being stalked," here he gave a nod to Jason, "I was worried about you and wondered if there was anything in your past that might help. But you are clean as a whistle."

"Well, this had all been fun, but I've had enough of Montreal and murder and don't plan to come back for a long time." And then I saw a look pass between Jason and Hugh.

Chapter 25

June was fast approaching and Montreal was in bloom everywhere I looked. I had packed up my belongings and cleaned the condo, knowing that the new owners would be moving in soon. I was surprised that it had sold so fast, but it was in a really nice area and the condo itself was lovely.

Tim was supposed to arrive soon and spend a day or two in Montreal before we went home for good. It was just as well that we had two cars because all my gear wouldn't fit in my little Mini Cooper. Jason was staying one more day and then heading out to Florida to meet my parents.

By noon time Hugh, Jason and I were sitting on the front steps waiting for Tim to arrive. He had called a few minutes earlier and said he was just getting into the city. Argus knew something was up and I swear he, too, knew that Tim was coming. Tim drove up and parked in front of the house. Argus went off in a tear to meet him and Tim came up the front walk carrying a squirming Argus in his arms.

"What the hell is all that?" I asked pointing to Tim's car. The car was filled with stuff. "You're supposed to be taking stuff away, not bringing in more stuff." By now I noticed that the three of them were arranged in front of me. Tim in the middle and one arm around Jason, who was now holding Argus, and another arm around Hugh.

"It must have slipped my mind," said Tim as the other two looked at me and laughed. "I'm the one who bought the condo."

"You *bought* the condo?"

"Yes, I did. I sold my house to Jessica and Derek and thought this would be nice to have for our vacations. The real estate agent is going to rent it out to short term business people when we aren't using it. It's a win-win situation."

"And you two knew about this?" I asked the other two. They just nodded.

"You three are a piece of work," I said and tried to frown, but of course I couldn't help laughing.

****

The Fourth of July is a big, big deal in Bath, Maine. There are American flags everywhere and the streets are decorated with red, white, and blue bunting. There is the parade and speeches in the park, a band concert, and family cookouts, and then fireworks at the end of the day.

Bath Iron Works has been turning out vessels for the navy longer than anyone can remember, and the launching of a new navy destroyer on the holiday made it extra special.

Tim and our two friends Jason Goulet and Billy Simpson were in charge of the backyard cookout. I had made the salads and desserts early in the day and was sitting back now in the shade with a cold beer.

Jason was coming to the cookout and this would be the first time he would get to meet everyone. He had only recently returned from Florida and claimed he had a great time with my parents. Since then he had been on a few job interviews, and now was looking forward to a peaceful summer before he returned to teaching in the fall.

Rhonda Shepard was the first to arrive wearing a 1950's sun dress and straw hat. She had her live-in guy, Jackson Bennett in tow. I was glad to see that he was dressed in regular clothes.

"Where's the kid?" she asked. "I can't wait to meet him."

"He's coming and I already warned him about you," I said.

"Asshole."

Tim's daughter Jessica and her husband Derek Cooper were next to arrive. They had just come from the parade and were giving Tim a rundown of what we missed.

Parker Reed came next with a case of beer. I'm not sure how many people he thought were coming, but a case seemed like overkill. Parker opened a beer for himself and then took a ginger ale over to Billy. Billy was still clean and sober after three years, and we all made sure to congratulate him.

"Bright Blessings, everyone!" I heard as Viola Vickner, our local Wiccan priestess, entered the backyard. Viola was wearing a long black dress with embroidered stars. She had on silver jewelry and flowers in her hair. She quickly spotted Pastor Mary Bailey and Rabbi Beth White and the three spiritual women gathered in one corner of the yard.

"Where's the caldron?" I asked as I walked by. Beth flipped me the bird.

"Is he here yet?" asked Monica. She opened a beer and sat down with me in the shade.

"Not yet."

"I love him already,' she said. "I just have that feeling, and the look on your face is more than enough for me."

Hugh Cartier had driven down from Montreal to experience his first Fourth of July. He gave me a wave from across the yard. Hugh was staying with Rhonda and Jackson and by all accounts enjoying his time in Bath.

I was amused to see Parker Reed make a beeline to Hugh and introduce himself. Billy Simpson caught the action and went over to drag Parker away. I was happy to see that Billy was becoming more assertive.

A van from the Sagadahoc Nursing Home pulled up at the curb. Tim rushed out to help Beatrice Lafond navigate her wheel chair into the back yard.

"Happy birthday, Mrs. Lafond," I said as I rushed over to give her a hug. Beatrice was our high school English teacher and the oldest living member of the Morse High School Alumni Association.

"I understand there might be a surprise guest here today," she said to me. I shot Tim a look.

"I might have mentioned Jason once or twice," he said.

More friends and neighbors arrived and there was a general buzz in the air as little groups formed and conversations evolved. Suddenly all conversation stopped and heads whipped around to see the newcomer. I went over to him, put my arm around him, and faced the group.

"Everybody, this is Jason" And bless them all they cheered and one by one introduced themselves and gave him a hug. Jason had never looked happier.

The burgers were ready, the salads put out, and people began to move toward the gazebo. Mary Bailey, Beth White, and Viola Vickner stepped up on the gazebo as the guests gathered around. The three women held hands and almost immediately the guests all joined hands and made a semi circle in front of the gazebo.

"Let us give thanks for the blessings of friends and family," began Beth White.

"And for the beauty of the earth and the riches of the universe," added Viola.

"And let us pray for the generations of the past who have lived and died so that we, on this day, can celebrate our own sense of place in history," concluded Mary Bailey. The gathering responded with a loud "amen." Mary beckoned to Jessica to come up the steps of the gazebo.

"First of all I want to thank my two dads for this wonderful cookout on this beautiful day. And I want to officially welcome the newest member of the family, Jason Campbell."

Jason got up and gave Jessica a hug and addressed the gathering. "Thank you all for making me feel so welcome. You'll never know how much that means to me. I not only found a family, but I found a community and a home. I have my own little announcement. Starting in September I'll be teaching English here at Morse High."

Someone let out a loud whoop, and I think it was me.

"Since we're making announcements," said Jessica. "Derek and I have one to make too." Derek stepped up on the stage. "Derek and I are going to have a baby!"

Tim looked pale for a moment and then he let out a whoop ran up and hugged his daughter.

****

The sun had left the sky and night was coming on, the backyard had been cleaned up and everything put away. Tim and I were sitting on the back porch watching the fireworks.

"Do you remember what I asked you last year?" asked Tim.

"You asked me if I believed in the power of love," I replied.

"And what's your answer this year."

I got up and stood behind his chair and ran my fingers through his hair.

"More than I ever thought possible, Tim, I believe in the power of love."

"Me too," said Tim reaching up to touch my face. "Me too."

Jesse's Recipes from Montreal

Canadian Bean Soup
A great hearty soup for a cold day

    1 pound sausage meat
    1 medium onion
    1 can great northern beans, rinsed and drained
    1 can diced tomatoes
    1 can chicken broth
    1 teaspoon Italian seasoning
    Salt and pepper

Brown the meat and onion in a fry pan. Place the ingredients into a crock pot and cook on low for six to eight hours.

Horiatiki: Greek Salad
    1 Cucumber
    1 Green pepper
    1 small onion
    6 black olives
    2 Tomatoes
    ¼ pound Feta cheese
    3 tablespoons olive oil
    Salt and pepper

Slice vegetables and arrange on plate. Pour olive oil over the salad and top with a feta cheese. Salt and pepper to taste.

Souvlaki

    1 pound pork loin
    1 lemon
    2 tablespoons olive oil
    ½ cup water
    Salt and pepper

Cut pork into one inch cubes. Make a marinade with the juice of the lemon, water, and olive oil. Let the meat marinate for at least one hour. Arrange meat on a stick or spear and cook over an open flame or barbecue grill.

Orange Beets

8 medium beets
1 cup orange juice
2 teaspoons corn starch
¼ cup honey
2 tablespoons butter

    Cook beets in water until tender. Peel and slice, and keep warm in a covered pan.

    In a saucepan combine orange juice, cornstarch, and honey, and beat with a fork until smooth. Bring to a boil and stir for two minutes. Add butter and stir until melted. Pour over beets.

Canadian Chicken Pot Pie

1 pound skinless, boneless cooked chicken breast halves – cubed

6 cooked link sausages cut into small pieces

1 cup sliced carrots

1 cup frozen green peas

1/3 cup butter

1 small chopped onion

1/3 cup all-purpose flour

1/2 teaspoon salt

1/4 teaspoon celery seed

1 3/4 cups chicken broth

2/3 cup milk

2 unbaked pie crusts

Preheat oven to 425 degrees. In a saucepan, combine carrots, and peas. Add water to cover and boil for 15 minutes. Remove from heat, drain and set aside. Add cooked chicken and sausage.

In another saucepan over medium heat, cook onions in butter until soft and translucent. Stir in flour, salt, pepper, and celery seed. Slowly stir in chicken broth and milk. Simmer over medium-low heat until thick. Remove from heat and set aside.

Cover pie plate with one pie crust and place the chicken and vegetable mixture in bottom. Pour hot liquid mixture over the meat. Cover with top crust. Make several small slits in the top.

Bake in the preheated oven for 30 to 35 minutes, or until pastry is golden brown and filling is bubbly. Cool for 10 minutes before serving.

New England Boiled Dinner

> 3 pounds corned beef
> 2 medium turnips peeled and cut up
> 6 large carrots
> 6 potatoes peeled and quartered
> 1 medium head of cabbage
> 1 bay leaf
> 6 pepper corns
> 3 whole cloves
> 6 whole beets

Cover corned beef with water, add bay leaf, pepper corns, and cloves. Bring to a boil. Cut heat back to a simmer and cook for three hours or until the meat is tender. Remove meat and let cool. Remove pepper corn and cloves.

Add potatoes, carrots, turnips, and cabbage to the water and cook until tender. Cook beets in a separate pan.

Arrange sliced corn beef and vegetables on a platter and serve.

The Maine version often substitutes smoked shoulder for corn beef.

The Canadian version adds split yellow peas, cooked in a mesh bag.

Honey Roasted Vegetables

    2 sweet potatoes, peeled and quartered
    3 carrots, peeled and thickly sliced
    ½ cup walnuts
    ¼ cup honey

Preheat oven to 375, Toss all the ingredients together and place in baking dish. Bake for one hour.

Coconut Upside-Down Cake

    6 tablespoons butter
    2/3 cup of brown sugar
    2 tablespoons water
    1 cup toasted coconut
    1 ¼ cup all purpose flour
    1 ¼ teaspoon baking powder
    ½ teaspoon salt
    ¼ cup butter
    1 egg
    ½ cup milk
    1 tablespoon vanilla extract

Spread coconut on baking sheet in a single layer and bake at 325 for five to six minutes until golden brown.

In a saucepan melt 6 tablespoons butter, brown sugar, and water. In an eight inch round cake pan spread the coconut and cover with the brown sugar mixture.

In a mixing bowl, cream butter and sugar, and egg. Add flour, baking powder, and salt and beat for one minute Pour batter over coconut mixture and bake at 350 for 35-40 minutes until done. Cool and turn upside down on plate.

205

12745769R10125

Made in the USA
Lexington, KY
26 December 2011